Pouncing on the Proof – A Norwegian Forest Cat Café Cozy Mystery – Book 14

by

Jinty James

Pouncing on the Proof – A Norwegian Forest Cat Café Cozy Mystery – Book 14

by

Jinty James

This is a work of fiction. All characters, names, places and events are the product of the author's imagination or used fictitiously.

ISBN: 9798476674085

DEDICATION

To my wonderful Mother, Annie,
and AJ

CHAPTER 1

"Would you look at this place!" Zoe Crenshaw craned her neck, looking up at the high ceiling, with decorative flat moldings painted in a pleasing shade of cream. The walls of the large room were painted in the same shade, with tasteful gold accents at the corners.

"I know," Lauren agreed with her cousin.

They'd just arrived at the reception venue her mother had requested they visit. Her mom had enthused about the place, telling her it would be perfect.

But was it perfect for her and Mitch?

She looked down at her engagement ring, the round brilliant diamond in its gold band sparkling in the July sunshine streaming through the glass paneled windows. She loved the ring she'd chosen. She loved Mitch. But …

"What is it?" Zoe glanced at her.

Lauren took in the perfection of the large room. The white and gold upholstered dining chairs, the podium, and above her, a large chandelier dripping with numerous crystal pendants.

"I don't know if it's really—"

"Hello, ladies." A fussy short man in his fifties bustled up to them. He consulted his clipboard. "Crenshaw party?"

"Yes," Lauren answered.

"I'm Reginald, owner and manager of this wonderful venue." He beamed. When they didn't say anything, he peered past them. "Is your fiancé accompanying you? Your mother told me over the phone that he would be here so we can go over everything together."

"Mitch will be here as soon as possible," Lauren replied.

"I'm Lauren's cousin, Zoe." Zoe smiled at him.

"Very good." He nodded. "Let's get started." He checked his gold timepiece. "I have another party arriving in thirty minutes. Your fiancé will just have to catch up when he gets here."

He ushered them over to a large polished mahogany table sporting a vase of red roses, and gestured to them to take a seat.

"Now, as you can see, this is a wonderful venue for a reception." He waved his hand around the large room, the polished wooden floorboards gleaming in the late afternoon sun. Although it was a warm day, it was cool inside the building, the air conditioning humming faintly.

Lauren thought it was like a little castle, or perhaps a miniature stately hall – hence its name, Stately Vue Hall. She could see why her mother had been so enthusiastic about holding the celebration here.

"It definitely is." Zoe nodded.

"How many guests will you have?" he asked.

Lauren blinked. "Umm…"

"She hasn't decided yet," Zoe said. "Neither has Mitch."

"That too," Zoe agreed.

"Any idea at all of numbers?" Reginald asked, his pen at the ready.

"Not really," Lauren admitted. "Not too big, though."

"Are cats allowed in here?" Zoe enquired.

"I'm afraid not." He shook his head.

"That means—" Zoe turned to her. "Annie won't be able to come."

"Annie?" He frowned.

"My Norwegian Forest Cat," Lauren told him.

"She works in the café with us," Zoe added. "The Norwegian Forest Cat Café in Gold Leaf Valley. It only took us thirty minutes to drive here."

Stately Vue Hall was conveniently situated halfway between Sacramento and their small town, another feature her mother had pointed out.

"No cats," he confirmed.

Her long-haired silver-gray tabby would be disappointed. She'd left Annie relaxing on the sofa at home after they closed the café early to arrive here on time.

But … would it actually be a good idea to have Annie at the reception no matter how small – or large – it would be? Her fur baby loved seating customers at the café, and joining her favorites at their tables, "talking" to them with her distinctive brrts and chirps, but would the crowd of people at the reception be too overwhelming for Annie? It was something she, Mitch, and Annie would need to discuss. Zoe as well.

"No cats. That's no good." Zoe furrowed her brow.

"Let's move on." He unclipped a sample menu and handed it to them. "We have different price options. For only thirty dollars per head, we have a two-course meal. A healthy green salad made with a variety of fresh lettuce leaves and cucumber, and a vegan pasta dish. We have vegans and vegetarians covered." He beamed.

"What about meat eaters?" Lauren asked. Mitch enjoyed a good steak.

"It will be interesting for them to have something different for one meal. Our pasta dish is divine!" He kissed his fingertips. "Little pasta shells with a simple tomato sugo that is out of this world, with a touch of fresh basil leaves. We do our best for our budget brides."

"Thirty dollars each is budget?" Zoe asked.

"Yes," he replied. "You will not find anyone else who treats their budget customers with as much respect as we do."

"We?" Lauren looked around the empty room.

"My assistant, Myrna. She was supposed to meet with you this afternoon, but she had to go to the dentist. She promised she'd be back as soon as possible."

As if on cue, a rear door opened and a bespectacled woman in her mid-thirties rushed over to them. Her dark hair was caught up in a bun and she wore a gray skirt and plain white blouse.

"I got back as fast as I could, Reginald," the newcomer said apologetically.

"This is my assistant, Myrna." He turned to her. "You might as well stay now. When the next party arrives, I must attend to them personally."

"Of course." Myrna nodded to him, then smiled at Lauren and Zoe. "Hello."

They returned her greeting.

Myrna sat down next to Reginald. "Where are we up to?" She brandished her own clipboard and pen.

"You don't have a tablet or a laptop?" Zoe's dark brown eyes were curious.

"No need for them," Reginald informed them. "I prefer things to be done the old-fashioned way."

"To the detriment of us all." A well-groomed woman in her fifties emerged from the rear. She wore a smart beige linen suit with the merest hint of pink in its shade, which suited her complexion and dark brown hair. "Hello, I'm Elizabeth, co-owner of this establishment. I'm happy to help you in any way I can."

"Thank you," Lauren replied, wondering if this meeting would have gotten off to a better start if Elizabeth had greeted them instead of Reginald.

"I have things well in hand, Elizabeth." Reginald frowned at her.

Elizabeth looked like she wanted to argue, then smoothed her expression. "Very well, *dear*, but I will be here when our next party arrives."

She nodded pleasantly to Lauren and Zoe, then left the room.

Reginald must have realized they were looking at him curiously. "Elizabeth is my ex-wife – and partner in our business."

"Oh." Lauren didn't know what else to say.

"Now." He rustled some papers on his clipboard. "We've gone over the budget meal option. For—"

"What about dessert?" Zoe asked. "Is dessert included in the thirty-dollar price point?"

"No," he replied. "That is what your wedding cake is for. If you do not have a preferred supplier for your cake, we can recommend one. The starting price for a one tier cake for fifty guests is three hundred and fifty dollars."

Lauren blinked at the price.

"What about beverages?" Zoe pressed. "Is champagne included for the toasts? Or—"

"No," he replied. "Sparkling water is provided for the meal. Our budget brides make their own arrangements for alcohol. Naturally, there is a corkage fee and we provide a licensed bartender for an extra charge. Or we can provide the champagne and anything else you desire, but for a price."

Naturally, Lauren thought. Her heart began to sink. Although it was beautiful, she didn't think this place was right for her – or Mitch – or Annie.

She didn't know how her mother would react. Since her parents were paying for most of the wedding, her mother had come up with some ideas of what she thought would be suitable. But she didn't think they were her or Mitch's idea of suitable. When he arrived, she'd talk to him.

"But don't despair." Reginald looked like he wanted to pat both of them on the hand. "For fifty dollars per head, you will receive champagne, wine for the meal, a delicious chicken entrée, and chocolate mousse for dessert."

"Fifty?" Lauren's voice was faint. If she and Mitch invited fifty people, that was already two thousand, five hundred dollars.

"Plus the venue fee of course," Reginald added. "That is one thousand dollars for six hours."

"How much is it for the budget package?" Zoe asked.

"The venue fee is the same, regardless of which menu you choose," he told her severely. "And if you want a longer reception, we're happy to accommodate you, at a price of one hundred dollars per extra hour."

"We should get into the wedding business." Zoe nudged her.

"So that's two thousand, five hundred dollars for six hours, the budget menu, and fifty guests," Lauren said.

"That is correct." He looked at her in approval. "And we have two more menus. The seventy-five-dollar menu features your choice of steak or seafood, endive salad, and a dessert bar. The one-hundred-dollar menu features a seafood entrée, steak or duck, dessert bar, and complimentary sugared almonds as bonbonnieres for your guests. There are vegan options as well."

Lauren didn't even want to think how much those packages would cost with fifty guests.

"Are you okay?" Zoe whispered. "You look a bit pale."

"I feel pale," she murmured.

Her parents wanted to pay for the wedding, but they hadn't specified a budget. Was her mother aware of how much this venue cost? She'd have to call her once she got home.

Reginald checked his watch, a frown on his face. "Is your fiancé coming this afternoon?"

"He said he'd be here," Lauren told him. And Mitch always kept his word.

"Yeah." Zoe nodded. "Mitch is a police detective. Sometimes he gets a bit held up."

"He'll call me if he can't make it." Lauren looked at her phone. No missed messages or texts. "He'll be here."

"Let's talk about dates." Reginald looked at the sheets of paper on his clipboard. "We are very popular, but I have one available date in the next six months. Three o'clock on a Tuesday afternoon. In October."

"We can't have the wedding for six months?" Lauren slumped back in her chair.

"You can have it in October." Reginald's pen was poised over his clipboard. "Let's pencil you in for this date, and we can decide on the menus later."

"I need to talk to Mitch about this first." Lauren found her voice.

"Yeah, people work on Tuesdays." Zoe frowned at Reginald. "We'd have to close the café, and Mitch would have to get time off work, plus everyone we're inviting would need to take the afternoon off." She turned to Lauren. "Does your Mom know about this?"

"I think she assumed it would be a weekend wedding." Like Lauren had.

"Yeah, Saturday would be better," Zoe agreed.

Reginald looked shocked. "All our Saturdays are booked until next year. If you wanted such a specific day, you should have contacted us a long time ago."

"But I've only been engaged for six months," Lauren protested. She touched the diamond in her ring and instantly felt better. Taking a deep breath, she said, "I'm sorry, but—"

"Have I missed anything?" A tall man strode into the large room. Lean and muscular, he wore fawn slacks and a white long-sleeved shirt. His dark brown hair was cut short, and his brown eyes looked serious.

"Not really." Lauren smiled at her fiancé, catching the faint scent of his light citrus aftershave.

"We were discussing dates," Zoe told him.

Mitch sat down beside her, nodding to Reginald and Myrna as they were introduced.

"The sooner the better, as far as I'm concerned." He captured Lauren's hand, and smiled tenderly at her.

Reginald cleared his throat. "As I was saying to your intended, that will not be possible. Unless you prefer a Tuesday afternoon."

"No," Mitch replied. "Sorry, but our friends work, and we wanted to invite them." He turned to Lauren. "Didn't we?"

"Of course." She nodded. They hadn't sorted out the guest list yet or had much of a conversation about exactly who to invite. They'd have to talk about it – perhaps tonight.

"We can pencil in a date later." Reginald made a note on his clipboard. "Now, I have gone over the menus, but I'd be happy to explain them to you."

"No need," Mitch replied. "Lauren can fill me in afterward. I want what she wants." He squeezed her hand.

"An admirable sentiment." Reginald nodded. "That leaves the question of the wedding cake. As I previously explained, if you do not have a preferred baker, we can recommend one. The price for a simple one tier to serve fifty guests starts at three-hundred and fifty dollars."

"You're undercharging for your cupcakes," Mitch whispered in her ear.

Lauren stifled a smile.

"We'll have to consider that," Zoe told Reginald. "We were thinking of having some tastings. Do you do that?"

"Of course." He nodded. "We can provide you with three samples from our recommended provider." He leafed through his papers and handed Zoe a sheet. "Here is all the information. Just call me when you're ready and I'll set it up."

Zoe scanned the paper. “It says there’s a charge.” She sounded indignant.

“You’ll find most things have a cost,” Reginald informed her, “especially when it comes to weddings.”

The roar of a high-performance car outside caught Lauren’s attention.

“Ah.” Reginald stood. “That must be our next client.” He nodded to them. “Let me know if you’re serious about having your reception here, and I’ll do everything I can to help. Good afternoon.” He bustled through the front entrance, no doubt wanting to greet the new arrival.

Elizabeth, the ex-wife, swept through from the rear.

“I couldn’t help overhearing, dear.” She spoke to Lauren. “If you really want to get married on a Saturday, I might be able to help.” She pulled out a little diary from her skirt pocket. “I have a cancellation list – Reginald probably forgot to mention that.” She shook her head. “He *is* getting a little older.”

"Yes, we are interested in a Saturday," Zoe said.

Lauren shot her *a look*.

"What? We – you – are," Zoe protested.

"We might need to think about it," Lauren replied.

"I'm happy with whatever you want," Mitch told her.

She smiled at him.

"What about a horse-drawn carriage?" Zoe asked Elizabeth. "Can you organize that?'

Elizabeth looked a little surprised but didn't hesitate. "Of course, my dear. Whatever your heart desires."

"I'm the one getting married." Lauren nudged her cousin in a teasing manner.

"I know that." Zoe grinned. "But it's only going to be once. Why not make it super special?"

Elizabeth looked at Zoe shrewdly. "If you ever want to work in the wedding industry, call me." She fished a card out of her pocket and handed it to her.

"Thanks." Zoe glanced at the card and put it in her purse.

"Now, let me put you down on the cancellation list." Elizabeth held her pen in the air.

Lauren looked at Mitch. He nodded.

"Okay." Wondering if she was doing the right thing, Lauren gave her name and phone number.

"Wonderful." Elizabeth smiled at her. "I'll be in touch if a Saturday crops up – and you'd be surprised at how many cancellations we get at the last minute."

"Really?" Zoe's eyes widened.

"Oh, yes. The bride discovers that the groom has cheated on her at his bachelor party, or the bride decides to run off with another man on the night of her bachelorette party."

"What happens then?" Mitch frowned.

"We call the next person on our list, and sometimes they can quickly organize their wedding guests and bring their wedding forward. We charge a non-refundable deposit when you book your date with us. Did Reginald mention that?"

"I don't believe he did," Lauren answered.

"Oh dear." Elizabeth tutted. "He *is* slipping. Never mind, I've told you now. Is there anything else I can help you with?"

"No, I don't think so. Thank you." Lauren just wanted to go outside in the fresh air, even if it was warm out there, and think things – and talk things – over with Mitch.

"Thank you for your help." Mitch smiled at her politely.

"Any time," Elizabeth told him.

She walked them toward the entrance, just as a pretty blonde girl entered, accompanied by a hearty-looking man. His prematurely graying tufts of hair were slicked back.

"George Montson. And this is my daughter Brianna." The man nodded to Elizabeth and Reginald. "We have an appointment."

"Oh, Daddy, it's perfect!" Brianna looked around twenty, her hair flowing in waves down her slender back. Her expertly cut white halter dress displayed her figure to advantage. White kitten heels, and a matching white handbag that probably cost more than a single tiered wedding cake, completed her outfit.

"Wow," Zoe muttered.

Lauren nodded.

"We'll have the orchestra over there." Brianna pointed to the far corner of the room. "Lots of flowers, of course, and a huge wedding cake, because I'll have so many guests, and–"

"How many guests?" Reginald looked ready to write down a figure.

"Three hundred, isn't that right, Daddy?"

"That's right." He smiled proudly. "Brianna's friends, our extended family, and my business associates."

"Of course, of course." Reginald looked delighted. "I've already sent the menu packages to your office.

Have you had a chance to look them over?"

"We'll have the most expensive one, won't we, Daddy?" Brianna looked at her father appealingly.

"Yes." Her dad nodded.

"Excellent." Reginald sounded gleeful.

Lauren calculated a cost of thirty thousand dollars. She looked at Mitch, who raised his eyebrow.

"Whoa," Zoe murmured.

"Now, what about the cake?" Reginald inquired. "We have connections with a wonderful baker who—"

"Can he make this?" Brianna whipped out her phone and practically shoved it into his face.

"Of course," he assured her. "He is a genius and can bake anything you desire. A five-tier cake with cascading pink rose sugar flowers is child's play to him."

"We'll need to have a tasting." Brianna made it sound like a warning.

"We usually charge for the tastings, but for you, my dear, it will be complimentary." Reginald beamed at her.

"It's not complimentary for us – you," Zoe muttered.

"Mmm." Lauren nodded.

"Now, which date were you thinking of?" Reginald asked. Elizabeth joined the three of them.

"Yes, dear, which date?"

"Saturday, August fourteenth," Brianna announced, as if expecting applause.

Reginald blanched.

"I'm afraid that's not possible. We're fully booked for the next six months. Unless you would like a Tuesday in October at three o'clock."

"That's *your* date." Zoe turned to Lauren, outraged.

"Except we didn't want it," Lauren reminded her.

"Oh, yeah." Zoe nodded.

"But I've told all my friends that's when I'm getting married!" Brianna looked like she wanted to stamp her foot. "It's my dream date! I *have* to get married on that day."

"Is there any way we can fix this?" Her father appealed to Reginald and Elizabeth. "Name your price. I can't have Brianna upset."

Reginald consulted his clipboard. "I'm afraid the other party paid for this date in full. I cannot cancel it."

"How much?" Brianna's dad pulled out his fancy leather wallet. "Ten thousand? More? Consider it a bonus."

Reginald looked affronted. "I'm afraid I cannot. If word got out, my whole business could be ruined."

"*Our* business, dear," Elizabeth reminded him. "The judge awarded me half, since I helped you buy this place and worked alongside you for *so* many years."

"You two are divorced?" Brianna's dad chuckled. "You seem like an old married couple."

"Unfortunately." Elizabeth frowned at her ex-husband. "It's a shame that California is a community property state. I try to make the best of things."

"If we can get back to the matter at hand." Reginald's tone was brusque.

"Now, you can have the first Saturday in February, or—"

"It has to be Saturday, August fourteenth." This time Brianna did stamp her well shod foot, her white kitten heel coming dangerously close to Reginald's black leather loafer.

"Let me put you on our cancellation list." Elizabeth whipped out her little book. "Just in case that day opens up." She made a note.

"Brianna is marrying Bobby," George said.

"This is Bobby." Brianna scrolled through her phone, then brandished it in Reginald's face, then showed Elizabeth. She turned to Lauren. "You can see, too." She seemed to notice Mitch for the first time, and gazed at him appreciatively.

Zoe crowded next to Lauren, as they glanced at an ordinary young man in his early twenties, with light brown hair. He looked a little stunned in the photo, as if he couldn't believe he was standing next to such a perfect goddess as Brianna, much less be engaged to her. But Brianna showed off her huge diamond ring in the image, a proud smile on her face.

Brianna suddenly gazed shrewdly at Lauren. “Is *her* wedding date on a Saturday? When is it?”

“I’m afraid I cannot divulge such sensitive information,” Reginald told her severely.

“I don’t have a date,” Lauren informed her.

“Not yet,” Zoe added.

“Oh.” Brianna’s expression fell.

Lauren guessed she was about to demand that day. Perhaps she was wrong.

“Well, sweetie, what do you want to do?” George asked his daughter.

“I’ve *got* to have my wedding here, Daddy. It’s absolutely *perfect*.” Brianna gazed at the decorative high ceilings. “Can you just imagine this space filled with pink roses?” She glanced at Lauren, Zoe, and Mitch. “That’s my signature flower.”

“Hmm. Maybe we need signature flowers,” Zoe mused. “Maybe mine should be lavender because I like purple. No, lilac, no—”

"We can talk about it later," Lauren said. "I just want to go home."

"Good idea." Zoe nodded.

They said goodbye to Reginald and Elizabeth, and made their way out to the bright sunshine, the crunch of gravel under their feet. Lauren could hear Brianna still arguing that she absolutely must have her dream date next month.

"Phew." Zoe theatrically mopped her brow, her brunette pixie bangs bouncing against her forehead.

"Do you want to wait for a Saturday here?" Mitch asked Lauren.

She looked up at him, taking in the concern in his brown eyes. She loved everything about him, not just his dark good looks, but the way he listened to her, was protective toward her, but realized she was her own person, and appreciated her independence.

"No. I don't think this place is really us, although it *is* beautiful." She admired the graceful architecture. "But Mom seemed keen on having the reception here."

"I hear you." He nodded. "If all this planning gets too much, we could always elope."

She wondered if he was joking, but the serious look on his face convinced her otherwise.

It was a tempting thought – just her and Mitch – unless Annie could somehow come to the secret ceremony as well, but …

"I think my parents would be disappointed if they weren't there."

After a moment, he nodded. "Mine would be, too."

"And Zoe, and our friends."

"Yeah. Chris is going to be my best man."

The paramedic, Mitch's closest friend, was dating Zoe.

"I'll call Mom when I get home and tell her that there aren't any dates available."

"Except for Tuesday." He smiled ruefully.

Lauren looked around, but her cousin had vanished.

"Let's go home." Mitch put his arm around her as they strolled to the cars. Zoe was already in the driver's seat of Lauren's white compact car.

"I thought I'd give you two some alone time," Zoe called out of the open window. "If you want to talk to Mitch on the way home, I can drive myself."

They agreed to do that, Lauren sliding into her fiancé's vehicle. Zoe waved goodbye, tooting the horn as she drove off.

"Is Zoe going to be your maid of honor?" Mitch started the engine.

"I need to talk to her about that. And we need to make a guest list, organize the cake, and I haven't even started looking for a dress yet." Her stomach clenched in panic. "As well as find somewhere to hold the reception."

"We could always hold it at the café," Mitch joked, accelerating away from the posh venue.

Lauren blinked. Could they?

CHAPTER 2

"Lauren, I want you to reconsider Stately Vue Hall." Her mother's voice came over the cell phone loud and clear. "It's just perfect for you – and all our guests."

Our?

"Don't worry about the cost. Your father and I have saved for years to give you a beautiful wedding. When I saw it featured in a magazine, I thought it would be perfect for you."

Lauren sat on the pink sofa in her living room, Annie nestled beside her, seeming to pay attention to Lauren's mother's voice sounding from the other end of the phone. Her green eyes widened and her furry gray ears pricked.

When Lauren had inherited her Gramm's Victorian cottage and attached café, she hadn't hesitated to leave her office job behind in Sacramento to run the café full time. Annie had accompanied her, and they'd changed the name to the Norwegian Forest Cat café.

Zoe had visited her one weekend to help out, and had enjoyed herself so much that she'd ditched her temp office jobs in San Francisco and moved into the cottage with them, becoming their right hand.

Lauren saw her mother a few times per year, but relished her life here in the small town.

"But I'm not sure if it's right for us – me and Mitch. We were thinking of a Saturday and there aren't any for six months—"

"You've only been engaged for six months," her mother interrupted. "Some couples take *years* to plan their wedding. Surely you can wait several months?" she paused. "Unless—"

"No," Lauren replied, quickly guessing what her mother was about to say, heat in her cheeks. "*Of course* we can wait. But—"

"You don't want to," her mother said.

"Yes."

Her mother sighed.

"Just do this one thing for me. Go back to the venue and keep an open mind. If you really don't care for it, then I won't push it."

"Alright. Thanks, Mom. I'll call them and set up another appointment."

"Thank you, dear. And ask Mitch to be there as well. Make sure he sees the benefits of Stately Vue Hall. The architecture is stunning, and it's such a convenient location, halfway between us and you, and just so pretty, with their large grounds, and their knot garden. Your wedding photos would look incredible against that backdrop."

"There's a knot garden?"

"You mean you and Zoe didn't stroll through the garden? Really, Lauren—"

"We did glimpse a garden behind the hall, but we spent all our time inside. And then another party arrived—"

"Well, just make sure you take a good look at the garden on your next visit. I'm sure that will change your mind. And if you don't want to wait for a Saturday in six months' time, I'm sure Mitch can take a day off work and you can close the café. I can make a Tuesday work on my end. Have you thought about your honeymoon yet? You are taking one?"

"Of course," she assured her mom. Another thing she had to discuss with Mitch. Saying yes to his marriage proposal was incredibly simple compared to planning the wedding.

"Brrt?" Annie asked when Lauren said goodbye to her mother.

"Mom wants us to have the reception at the posh place." She stroked the feline's velvety soft fur, instantly feeling better. "When Mitch and I get married."

"Brrt?" Annie bunted her hand.

"Yes, you'll be part of it." Lauren smiled down at her. She couldn't imagine Annie not being included in the ceremony somehow. After all, her fur baby was in large part responsible for how she'd met Mitch in the first place. He'd entered the café, looking for Annie, as someone had told him to talk to her in regard to a crime that had occurred. She giggled, remembering Mitch's face when she'd informed him that Annie was her cat.

Their relationship had progressed slowly from there – and now they were about to get married! – if they could organize everything.

"I guess I'd better call Reginald and see if I can make another appointment to look around again with Mitch." Lauren reached for her phone.

"Who are you talking to?" Zoe zoomed into the living room. She grinned when she saw the two of them on the sofa. "Say no more."

Lauren explained that she'd promised her mother to give Stately Vue Hall a second chance.

"Cool. I'll come too. Maybe we can go on Monday when the café is closed."

"I'll check right now." Lauren made the call, Reginald sounding delighted.

Lauren put down her phone.

"All set for Monday morning." She crinkled her brow. "I hope Mitch can get some time off work."

"With all the overtime he does, they shouldn't have a problem giving him a couple of hours off."

"Do you want to come with us, Annie?" Lauren looked down at her. "Mom wants us to check out the knot garden."

"There's a knot garden?" Zoe's eyebrows climbed up her forehead. "I didn't see it today."

"Me either. But Mom said it would be a great setting for photos."

"Okay, we have to check it out *now*." Zoe grinned. "Ooh, we could visit Mrs. Finch afterward, and tell her all about it."

"She'd like that."

The elderly lady was one of their most regular customers, and a good friend.

"Brrt!" Annie's eyes sparkled at the mention of one of her favorite people.

"It's craft club tomorrow," Lauren reminded them. On Friday evenings, the three of them visited Mrs. Finch with their various projects. Zoe had investigated knitting, crochet, bead jewelry, string-art, and was currently engrossed in pottery. She made mugs with Annie's picture on them and sold them at the café to their loyal customers. They'd also started using them in the coffee shop as well.

Lauren had stuck with knitting, but had recently tried sewing, something which made Zoe shudder. After making two pink cushion covers to match their newish sofa, Lauren had taken a break, and was back to knitting Zoe a scarf. It might be ready for Christmas.

"Awesome. We can fill in Mrs. Finch about today's adventure. And tell her all about that spoiled bride – what was her name – Brianna?" Zoe tapped her cheek.

"I wonder if she *will* get her dream date on Saturday, August fourteenth," Lauren mused.

"Yeah, I wouldn't like to cross that girl." Zoe shuddered.

"Mitch is coming over tonight." Lauren checked her practical white wristwatch. “Is it nearly seven already?”

“Is he cooking?”

“No. We’re going to order pizza. Would you like to join us?”

“You know I never turn down pizza, but I’m meeting Chris at Gary’s Burger Diner.”

“Brrt?” Annie looked hopefully at Zoe.

“You know I’ll bring you back a plain burger.” She winked at the silver-gray tabby.

“Brrt!” *Thank you.*

“Wait until I tell Chris about this afternoon.” Zoe giggled. “I still think you should consider a horse-drawn carriage. I bet Aunt Celia would be pleased.”

“I think she would be.” Lauren smiled.

“I wonder if bridezilla Brianna has thought of that? Maybe she knows where to hire one!”

***

"We need to make a guest list," Lauren said an hour later. Mitch and the pizza had arrived, and now they were enjoying a simple dessert of chocolate ice cream.

"Okay."

"Brrt?" Annie sat next to Lauren at the kitchen table.

"I'll put your name down first." Lauren smiled at her fur baby. She made a note on the large piece of paper next to her.

"Your parents, and my parents," Mitch said.

"And Zoe, and Chris."

"Who else?" Mitch frowned.

"Any other family?"

"I guess a couple of cousins I haven't seen for years."

Lauren wrote that down.

"Friends?" she prompted.

"A few guys from Sacramento who are on the force there. I've been so busy, I haven't caught up with them lately."

"I understand." Annie and Zoe were her besties. She realized she'd lost contact with the friends she'd had in

Sacramento, before she moved to Gold Leaf Valley. But she'd been busy too, with running the café and "sleuthing" as Zoe liked to call it. So far, they'd helped solve thirteen murders. And some of their patrons had become their friends.

"What about your regulars, like Mrs. Finch?" he asked.

"Yes, we must invite her." Lauren wrote down her name. "And Martha, and little Molly and her mom Claire, and her husband. Are you okay with children at the wedding?"

"Of course." He smiled. "We're going to have kids of our own, right?"

"I hope so." She felt like blushing. Although Mitch stayed overnight at times, they hadn't really spoken about having children. But it was good to talk about this before the ceremony.

"Do you want to get married in Father Mike's church?" she asked. They were sporadic attendees at the local Episcopalian church.

"I'd like that." He looked at her tenderly.

“Me too. We’ll have to check with Father Mike to see if he has any vacancies.” After discovering that the reception venue was fully booked for six months apart from one Tuesday, she didn’t want to assume *anyone’s* availability.

A thought struck her.

“I haven’t spoken to Mom about who is going to marry us. She was saying today that the venue we saw this afternoon was the perfect distance between Sacramento and here.” She’d filled Mitch in when he’d arrived for dinner about her promise to take a second look at Stately Vue Hall.

“If we want Father Mike, maybe he’d be willing to marry us there, if we decide to go that way,” he offered.

“Thanks.” She reached for his hand across the table. “I just hope I’m not going to turn into a bridezilla.”

“You? No way. You’re nothing like that girl we met this afternoon.” He shuddered. “If she’s like that when she’s *not* planning her wedding, I don’t think her marriage will last long.”

"We still need to decide on a cake, flowers, and my dress. And your outfit. And Chris's. And Zoe's."

"Brrt!" *And mine!*

They both chuckled affectionately at Annie's declaration.

"That's right," Lauren murmured to her fur baby. "And yours." She sighed. "There's just so much to do."

"You know I'll help you any way I can."

"I know." She relished the feel of her hand in his. "We haven't even decided on a date – not really."

"The sooner the better. Why don't I call Father Mike tomorrow and ask him about dates? And if he'd be willing to marry us at the posh place, if that's what you want."

"That would be great. Although, I'd rather get married in the church here." The white, clapboard Victorian church was homey and quaint, with a welcoming air. She felt more comfortable there than at Stately Vue Hall.

"Me too."

They smiled in perfect understanding.

They added a few more names to their guest list, then Mitch left. He was going to put in a couple of extra hours the next day, so he could get time off on Monday morning for their second visit to the elegant venue.

"Have you got everything sorted out?" Zoe asked when she came home a little later. She brandished a brown paper bag that smelled deliciously meaty. "Look what I've got for you, Annie. Fresh off the grill."

"Brrt!" Annie stood on her hind legs, her front paws patting the bag.

"Supper," Lauren told Annie. "Then I guess I'd better go to sleep." She yawned.

"Yeah, it's been a busy day," Zoe agreed.

After Annie enjoyed her plain burger patty, the trio got ready for bed. Annie curled up next to Lauren, while Zoe waved goodnight and headed to her bedroom.

It took a while for her to fall asleep. Invitation lists, flowers, and bridal dresses danced through her head until she didn't want to think about anything wedding related – at least for the next eight hours.

CHAPTER 3

While Lauren and Zoe readied the café the next morning, Mitch called with good news – Father Mike said he would be delighted to officiate at their ceremony, wherever they'd like to hold it.

"Woo hoo!" Zoe high-fived her when Lauren ended the call. "That's one thing we – you – don't have to worry about now."

"Yes." Lauren smiled. "Now all I *do* have to worry about, apart from all the wedding preparations, is coming up with a new cupcake flavor." She hadn't thought up one in a while and didn't want her customers tiring of her current offerings.

She turned to Zoe. "Got any ideas?"

"You already make lavender, lemon meringue – my current fave – lemon poppyseed, mocha, Norwegian apple, red velvet, salted caramel, super vanilla, and triple chocolate ganache."

Zoe tapped her cheek. "I've probably missed a couple."

An idea suddenly popped into Lauren's head. "What about carrot cake?"

"With lots of cream cheese frosting?"

"Brrt!" Annie agreed from her pink bed.

"I can make a batch on the weekend and see how they turn out." Since they were taking a second look at the reception venue on Monday and visiting Mrs. Finch, Saturday afternoon or Sunday would be the perfect time to experiment.

"Are you seeing Mitch on the weekend?" Zoe wanted to know.

"Only for more wedding planning. He's coming over on Sunday."

"Have you decided on your flower girls and – ahem – maid of honor?" Zoe looked at her expectantly.

"Brrt!" *Yes!* Annie trotted toward them, the expression on her face identical to Zoe's.

"I wanted to talk to both of you about that." Lauren looked at her two best friends. "Would you both be happy being co-maids of honor?"

Annie looked at Zoe, a smile tilting up her mouth.

"Brrt!" *Yes!*

"What Annie said." Zoe grinned. "I would be honored." She giggled at the pun. "We both would be, isn't that right, Annie?"

"Brrt!" *Yes!*

"We can walk down the aisle together. And wear matching flower headbands. With cat safe flowers, of course," Zoe added hastily.

Lauren smiled at the thought of them doing that. She blinked back sudden tears – happy ones.

"Thank you." She felt like the one who was honored.

"Your wedding is going to be awesome – you'll see."

"Brrt!"

***

After they opened at nine-thirty, their regular customers arrived.

"How are the wedding preparations?" Ms. Tobin asked, glancing around the café.

The interior walls were pale yellow, and the furniture consisted of pine tables and chairs. A string-art picture of a cupcake with lots of pink frosting decorated one of the walls – evidence of one of Zoe's hobbies.

"We've just started," Lauren replied.

"Brrt!" Annie trotted to greet the tall, slim fifty-something woman at the *Please Wait to be Seated* sign.

"You must tell me all about it, Annie." Ms. Tobin smiled down at the silver-gray tabby.

"Brrt." *I will.* She led her to a two-seater near the counter.

Ms. Tobin used to be their prickliest customer, but ever since Lauren and Zoe had saved her from an internet scam, she'd mellowed, and had become one of their most loyal patrons.

"How is your kitten Miranda?" Lauren asked, coming over. Zoe followed. Ms. Tobin had adopted the calico cat when the café had hosted an adoption day – in fact, Annie had made the match.

"She did the cutest thing the other day." Ms. Tobin shook her head in amusement. "I was about to put on my shoe, when I noticed one of her balls in it!"

"Maybe she was sharing her toy with you," Zoe suggested.

"I think so." Ms. Tobin nodded. "I called her and we had a lovely game for a few minutes – I rolled the ball on the carpet and she chased after it and batted it back to me." Ms. Tobin smiled at the memory, and turned to the silver-gray tabby. "Thank you again, Annie, for choosing Miranda for me."

"Brrt." *You're welcome.*

"Have you started on the guest list yet, Lauren?" Ms. Tobin asked.

"Last night," she replied.

"Is it going to be a big wedding? Or a small one?"

"We haven't quite decided yet," Lauren replied apologetically.

"We're still looking for somewhere to hold it," Zoe informed her.

They told her about their impending second visit to Stately Vue Hall.

"Oh, I think I read about that place in a magazine," Ms. Tobin enthused. "It looked beautiful."

"Maybe that's the same magazine Mom saw it in," Lauren replied.

"You must update me with your wedding plans."

Lauren promised to do so, wishing she could tell her that she was invited to the wedding, but the guest list wasn't completed, and they had to decide on a venue, and exactly where they would get married.

After they took Ms. Tobin's order of a large latte and a salted caramel cupcake, they headed back to the counter, Annie staying with her.

"Are you going to invite Ed?" Zoe whispered.

"Of course." Ed was her talented pastry chef and friend, who made mouthwatering Danish pastries. Although Lauren prided herself on her cupcakes, she knew her pastry wasn't as tender and flaky as Ed's.

"What sort of invites are you going to have? Emails? Or fancy paper? Or cardstock?"

Lauren stared at her cousin, panic clenching her stomach.

"I hadn't even thought of that."

"That could be my first duty as your co-maid of honor." Zoe's eyes sparkled. "I can find samples of each and show you."

"That would be great. But I don't think Mom would approve of emailed invitations."

"Yeah." Zoe nodded. "And I'm not sure if all our customers have an email address."

People of all ages visited the café, but a lot of their regulars were seniors, although some wielded their cell phones like professionals.

"I wonder if Mrs. Finch has an email address," Zoe mused.

"I can't remember her mentioning it," Lauren replied.

"We can ask her tonight!"

***

"So this afternoon when we weren't busy I looked on my phone and found some invitation options for Lauren," Zoe concluded.

The trio were gathered in Mrs. Finch's living room, decorated in shades of fawn and beige.

"Have you decided on a design yet, Lauren?" Their elderly friend peered at them through her spectacles as she sat in her comfortable chair. Her gray hair was piled on top of her head in a bun, a couple of wisps escaping, and she wore a green cotton skirt and white short-sleeved blouse.

Annie kept her company, perching on the fawn arm.

"Not yet. I can't decide between pink orchids, violets, abstracts, watercolors, and a whole lot of others. But you're invited, of course." She smiled at their friend.

Pleasure flickered across Mrs. Finch's face.

"Thank you, dear. Something lovely to look forward to."

"Do you have an email address?" Zoe asked.

"No. My friends call me or send me letters."

"That's good to know." Zoe made a note on her phone. "We'll give you another update on Monday afternoon. We're checking out Stately Vue Hall again." Zoe brought her up to date, telling her all about the spoiled bride Brianna.

"Maybe you'll find out if she did get her Saturday dream date in August after all," Mrs. Finch suggested.

"Brrt!"

The evening passed quickly, Lauren showing their friend Zoe's scarf in progress. Since her cousin had bought the red and purple self-striping yarn and asked Lauren to knit it for her, it wasn't a secret.

"And what about your pottery mugs, Zoe?" Mrs. Finch enquired.

"All this wedding talk has given me the most awesome idea! Annie in her co-maid of honor flowered headband as my new design."

"Brrt!" *Yes!* Annie's green eyes sparkled.

"That sounds amazing." Lauren smiled at her cousin.

"What if I make mugs for all the guests to take home as a gift? I could write Lauren and Mitch, and the date on one side, and Annie's co-maid of honor picture on the other." Zoe's face was alight with anticipation.

"I'd love that!" Lauren was sure her excitement mirrored Zoe's. Her cousin had discovered a talent for sketching while drawing Annie on her series of mugs.

"It sounds wonderful, Zoe," Mrs. Finch praised. "You must let me buy one from you. I'm not sure how much all your equipment and clay costs, but it can't be cheap."

"But you'll be our guest." Lauren sounded shocked.

"Yes. I want to give you one." Zoe beamed at their friend. "And this could be my wedding gift to Lauren and Mitch!"

"Brrt!"

"Well, if you're sure." Mrs. Finch wrinkled her brow a tad.

"The pottery studio doesn't charge that much to work there, and I can buy the clay in bulk," Zoe explained. "The most I'll spend is my time making the mugs, and glazing them. And painting in the details."

"It will be an amazing wedding gift." Lauren touched her cousin's arm. "Thank you. I'm sure Mitch will appreciate it as well."

"I hope so."

After they made Mrs. Finch a little latte with her capsule machine, they said goodbye.

"We'll see you on Monday if you don't pop into the cafe tomorrow morning," Lauren promised.

"Brrt!"

CHAPTER 4

The next morning, the café was busy with Saturday morning customers. Ed didn't work that day, so it was up to Lauren to make enough cupcakes to satisfy everyone.

"Phew!" Zoe theatrically mopped her brow when they finally closed at lunchtime. "We're sold out."

"I forgot to put some aside for us." Lauren shook her head in dismay.

"Never mind. You're making your new carrot cakes this afternoon – aren't you?" Zoe looked hopeful.

"Brrt?" *Aren't you?*

"Yes." Lauren smiled. "Would you like to help me, Annie?"

"Brrt!" *Yes!*

"And I'll work on the design for your wedding mugs. Just don't elope or something, because I'll need time to make the mugs, like I explained to Mrs. Finch last night."

"I won't," Lauren promised, wondering if somehow her cousin had overheard her conversation with Mitch outside Stately Vue Hall on Thursday afternoon. "I don't think Mom would be happy if we did that, anyway."

"Yeah. Oh – have you got my parents on the guest list?"

"Yes." She'd thought of it late last night and scribbled a note to herself. Perhaps she should keep the list next to her bedside table, or a journal where she could jot down ideas that came to her – at any time of the day or night.

They closed the café, cleaned up, and trooped along the private hallway that connected the coffee shop to the cottage.

After a quick lunch, Lauren set to work in the kitchen.

Zoe said she was going to stretch out on the sofa in the living room with a sketch pad.

Lauren gathered the ingredients together, and a large mixing bowl.

"Brrt?" Annie looked with interest at the carrots, raisins, and jars of spices on the table.

"We're going to make carrot cakes with a cream cheese frosting," she told her fur baby. "And if they're good, I can start making them for the café."

"Brrp." Annie sounded approving.

Lauren hummed as she mixed up the ingredients, including Ceylon cinnamon, freshly grated nutmeg, walnuts, and brown sugar. Annie seemed to enjoy hearing the little tune.

Lauren placed the cupcake tray in the oven. She could have used the commercial kitchen in the café, but cats weren't allowed in that part of the business, and it was fun having Annie as her 'supervisor'.

"Now we wait for them to bake," she told her fur baby. "Meanwhile, we can mix up the frosting."

Annie watched while she took out cream cheese from the fridge, along with butter, powdered sugar, and vanilla extract.

"Something smells yummy," Zoe called out from the living room, when the cupcakes were nearly done.

"Thanks." Lauren's mouth watered at the aroma wafting from the oven – carrot, raisins, cinnamon, and nutmeg. Although it hadn't been long since lunch, her stomach rumbled.

The timer dinged, and she took the tray out of the oven. Perfectly risen cupcakes greeted her – and Annie.

"Brrt." Annie seemed to nod in approval as Lauren placed the orange-brown goodies on a wire rack.

"We'll wait for them to cool," Lauren remarked. "And then we'll frost them."

"Brrt!" Annie jumped down from the chair and scampered toward the living room.

"Are they ready?" Zoe appeared in the doorway. "Annie alerted me."

"Just about." Lauren gestured to the treats. "They might still be a bit warm but—"

"I'll risk it." Zoe snatched one up and bit into it. "Mmm – oww! Hoth," she mumbled. After she swallowed, she blew on the remains. "You did warn me." She eyed the bowl of frosting on the table. "Are you going to frost them now?"

"When they've cooled down," Lauren replied in amusement. "I want to put some away for Mitch tomorrow, even though they won't be freshly baked."

"I'm sure he won't mind. Guys."

Lauren agreed with a smile.

She frosted the cupcakes when they'd cooled down, and she and Zoe enjoyed a latte with them. Annie joined them, looking from one plate to the other.

"I don't know if these would be good for you," Lauren apologized. "I'm sorry."

"Brrp." Annie's lower lip stuck out a little.

"What about some chicken in gravy?" Lauren headed to the pantry and got out one of Annie's favorites.

"Brrt!" Annie hopped down from the chair and sat next to her food bowl. When Lauren spooned the food into the lilac bowl, Annie tested the mixture with her little pink tongue, before lapping at it enthusiastically.

"Are you seeing Mitch tonight?" Zoe asked.

"No. Tomorrow. He said he wants to tidy up his apartment a bit. He's thinking of having his parents stay there when they come for the wedding, and he'll bunk in with Chris." Mitch's parents lived in San Diego.

"Good idea." Zoe nodded.

Chris lived in a scarce rental nearby. Although the outside of Chris's home was in need of some love, the interior was decent. Zoe had enjoyed adding some of her decorating touches to it, including some of her string-art pictures.

"Chris is working tonight." Zoe made a face. "But the three of us can watch something on TV."

"Brrt!" Annie seemed to like that idea.

"How's your sketch coming along?" Lauren asked, noticing the pad in Zoe's hand.

"Pretty good." Zoe held it out to her.

Lauren and Mitch was written in a graceful but easy to read script, and the date listed as *month day year*. Underneath was a drawing of Annie's furry face wearing a pretty floral headband.

"Your names will be on one side of the mug, and Annie will be on the other. I looked up cat safe flowers, and they include gerberas, pansies, orchids, and roses, and so I drew those on Annie's headband, but I don't know if they'll be in bloom for your wedding day. Once we know your exact date, I can put that in the design. Hmm." Zoe scrunched her brow. "I'll need to know how many guests are attending so I can make enough mugs, plus some spares just in case there are some accidents."

"Will you make more for the café as well?" Lauren asked. "I'll pay you for those. I'm sure our regulars would love to see them when they visit, whether they come to the wedding or not."

"Of course." Zoe sounded enthused. "But you don't have to *pay* me."

"Of course I do," Lauren said firmly. "It's a business expense. And it will be the café who pays you."

If there wasn't enough money in the coffers, she'd lend it to the business personally and pay herself back over time. But she knew the café account had a decent balance in it at the moment.

"Just let me know how much the café mugs will be. And include your time."

"You're the best." Zoe beamed. "And don't forget, the wedding mugs are my gift to you – and Mitch."

"I won't."

"Brrt!"

CHAPTER 5

Lauren spent a pleasant Sunday with Mitch. He loved the carrot cupcakes she'd saved for him, and they went over the guest list, finalizing it, with a total of fifty-three guests, including the café regulars who had become their friends.

Zoe spent the day with Chris, returning in the evening. Her face lit up when Lauren handed her the guest list.

"Awesome! Now all I need is the date to paint on the pottery mugs."

"We're working on it," Lauren reminded her.

"Is Mitch coming with us tomorrow to check out Stately Vue Hall again?"

She shook her head. "He still has to put in a couple of hours before he can get away. He'll meet us there."

Mitch had been apologetic about his work schedule. She understood.

"It's a shame Chris can't be there, too. But he's got a shift tomorrow." Zoe made a face.

They decided on an early night. Tomorrow was going to be busy for Lauren – after checking out the knot garden, they were going to visit Mrs. Finch, and then she wanted to mix up cupcake batter in readiness for Tuesday, when they opened the café. Plus a myriad of wedding related things to think about, such as the invitations.

Zoe had sent her a copy of the samples she'd found online, and Lauren had shown them to Mitch. He said he was happy with whatever she decided. Now she just had to choose.

Checking that a notepad was beside her alarm clock, she snuggled into bed with Annie. She dreamed of walking down the aisle to meet Mitch.

***

"Oh, excuse me." Lauren stood aside to allow Brianna, the bridezilla from last week, pass by her in the parking lot of the reception venue.

The father and daughter had just emerged from the stately building.

"Daddy, I must have my wedding here." She clung to his arm. "The flowers Reginald showed us were so beautiful. I *must* have my wedding *here*!"

"Didn't see you there." George, Brianna's dad, nodded to them, walking past. He looked business-like in dark gray slacks and a pale blue shirt.

"Where's your fiancé?" Brianna's gaze sharpened, and she paused.

"On his way," Lauren replied.

"Oh." Brianna sounded disappointed, then blinked as she noticed Annie. "You have a cat!"

"Her name is Annie," Lauren said.

"Brrt," Annie greeted her politely. Today, Brianna wore a summery pink frock that must have cost a fortune, and made Lauren feel that her apricot dress that she'd been pleased with that morning had suddenly turned into a frumpfest.

The heady scent of roses wafted from Brianna.

"Daddy, I want a cat like that." The girl pointed to Annie.

"I thought you wanted to marry Bobby," her dad replied.

"Yes, and now I want a cat as well. Just like this one."

"We'll see," he replied. "Excuse us." He nodded to them, and made his way to a fancy black sportscar parked a few spaces away from Lauren's. There were no other cars in the lot.

Lauren watched them drive away with a roar.

"No wonder your Mom wanted you to have the wedding here." Zoe's eyes widened as they walked into the large knot garden.

Small and large squares of green box hedge formed fancy designs, with flowering shrubs in the middle of each square. The gravel path curved around a corner.

"Brrt!" Annie looked around in approval. She wore her lavender harness.

"It *is* beautiful," Lauren agreed. She could just imagine her, Mitch, and Annie having their photos taken in here. The sweet birdsong in the distance added to the magic.

They'd arrived early, fifteen minutes ahead of their appointment, so they could have a good look around on their own, without any pressure from Reginald.

"Do you think we should let Reginald or his assistant Myrna know we're here?" Lauren asked after a few minutes of strolling through the garden, the scent of roses perfuming the air.

"Or his ex-wife Elizabeth," Zoe added. "Good idea."

"Brrp," Annie replied, leading the way to a particularly delightful red rose.

The weather wasn't as warm as it had been last Thursday, but Lauren began to feel hot. She'd rubbed on plenty of sunscreen on her bare arms, thinking her outfit of a lightweight apricot dress cut to flatter her curves was an appropriate choice for the morning. She and Zoe usually wore capris and a t-shirt as work attire during the summer, and jeans and sweaters in winter.

Zoe had dressed up a little for this meeting as well, with lavender capris and a white top with the merest hint of a ruffle, which suited her slim figure. The colors complimented her brunette hair.

"Did I say I love your outfit?" Lauren glanced at her cousin.

"Brrt!" Annie agreed.

"Thanks." Zoe grinned. "It's cool and comfy and a bit smart – but still me. Hmm, maybe I'll get married in it one day."

"Are you and Chris …" Lauren held her breath. Her cousin was pretty private about her relationship with Chris, one of the few things she was close-mouthed about.

"No," Zoe replied hastily. "At least, not yet. But ..." she sighed which was unlike her. "It would be nice one day. I guess."

Lauren knew her cousin well enough to realize that *I guess* was totally unnecessary.

"I hope I'll be your maid of honor – or should that be matron of honor?" she teased. "If you two get married after us."

"Brrt?" Annie asked hopefully, looking up at Zoe.

"Of course you'll be my maids or matrons of honor – both of you," she replied. "If it ever happens."

Lauren touched her cousin's shoulder in reassurance. She'd thought for a while now that Chris and Zoe were perfect for each other. Chris's easygoing, laid-back nature was an excellent foil for Zoe's good-hearted impulsivity. And Chris was a genuinely nice guy.

"We'd better go inside." Lauren looked at her watch. "Maybe we can check out the other part of the knot garden after our meeting." She gestured to the part that curved around the corner, hidden from view.

"I hope they allow Annie inside."

"Brrt!" *Yes!*

“If they don’t, we can have the meeting outside,” Lauren said firmly. Although she appreciated the beauty of the garden, and would love to have her wedding photos taken here, she didn’t think the rest of the venue was quite her – or Mitch – or Annie – or Zoe.

“So, have you changed your mind about having the reception here?” Zoe asked.

“Maybe I should wait for Mitch before I answer that.”

A loud scream pierced the serenity.

Lauren and Zoe looked at each other with wide eyes.

“Brrt?”

“What was—”

Another loud scream interrupted Zoe.

“It’s coming from over there!” Zoe pointed to the hidden part of the garden they hadn’t explored.

They ran toward the sound, Annie in the lead. They stopped in their tracks at the sight of Myrna pointing to a pair of trouser-clad legs sticking upside down in one of the square hedges, his feet shod in polished black loafers.

"It – it must be Reginald," Myrna gasped. "I was looking for him because I knew you had an appointment with him."

"We need to check if he's alive," Lauren said, wondering how on earth they could do it without disturbing the scene too much.

Zoe picked up a pair of pruning shears lying on the ground. "Maybe we can do it this way." She bent down and hacked away part of the hedge closest to the ground. It was damp, as if the garden had recently been watered and hadn't yet dried in the summer temperatures.

"I can see his face!" She peered through the branches.

"I think I've got a mirror." Lauren rummaged through her small purse. "Here's my compact."

"Eww." Zoe froze in her bent position.

"Brrt?" Annie joined her.

"Reginald's got flowers stuffed in his nose and mouth. And a trickle of blood down his cheek." Zoe wiggled her arm through the hole she'd made in the five-foot-tall box hedge. When she pulled her arm out, she looked at the shiny surface doubtfully. "I can't see any breath on it."

Lauren peered over her shoulder. The small mirror gleamed in the sunshine, but her cousin was right.

"What are we going to do?" Myrna shifted from one foot to the other. "He *can't* be dead!"

"We'll call for help." Lauren pulled her phone out of her purse.

Thankfully, the sound of sirens reached them in a few minutes.

They retreated to the shade of a small tree, where they could still keep watch over Reginald's body. A statue of a graceful roman woman, tastefully clad, kept them company.

Lauren watched as the authorities took over the scene.

"Lauren?" Mitch's voice.

"Brrt!"

"Mitch!" Relief flooded through her as he strode up to her, looking calm and capable in fawn slacks and a button-down white shirt.

"What's wrong? Are you okay?" He cupped her shoulders, looking at her intently, then at the paramedics working on Reginald – to no avail – having removed him from the hedge.

Shakily, she told him what had just happened, Annie interrupting with a series of brrts.

Zoe added that they'd bumped into spoiled bride Brianna and her father George when they arrived.

"Where's Elizabeth?" Mitch's gaze sharpened.

Lauren realized she hadn't seen Reginald's ex-wife.

"Reginald!" They heard a female voice coming closer. "Where are you? You'll be late for the next appointment."

Elizabeth rounded a hedge and halted when she saw everyone. Her gaze flickered to the paramedics, her eyes widening in shock.

"What's going on?"

"Ma'am, I'm afraid I have some bad news for you," Mitch began. "Perhaps we should sit down somewhere."

Elizabeth's gaze swung to Myrna, then to the rest of them.

"Reginald?" Elizabeth put her a hand to her mouth. "No, it can't be!"

"I'm afraid it is."

"What's going on?" Lauren heard Detective Castern's voice and inwardly shuddered.

"Not *him,"* Zoe muttered.

"What are you two doing here?" the middle-aged detective scowled at them. He did not get along with Mitch – or anyone else. Unfortunately, they both worked at the department in Gold Leaf Valley.

He noticed Mitch. "Denman. What are you doing here?"

"Castern." Mitch nodded. "I had an appointment here with my fiancée."

"We're potential clients," Zoe told him.

"And I suppose you called 911." He glared at Zoe.

"That's right. We did."

"I'll speak to each of you separately." He turned to Elizabeth. "Are you the owner? I'll need somewhere to question all the witnesses."

"You can use one of the reception rooms," Elizabeth told him in a shaky voice.

"You'd better show me." Castern escorted her toward the building. "I want all of you to come inside so you don't contaminate the scene." He ignored Annie.

Zoe rolled her eyes. "How can you stand working with him?" she muttered to Mitch.

"Some days are harder than others when we're both in the office," he admitted. "But I enjoy putting bad guys away."

"It's a shame you can't put *him* away."

Lauren stifled a smile.

"Brrt!"

Once they entered the stately building, Detective Castern took over the main reception room, leaving the four of them waiting in the hall, along with Myrna.

"I don't know how this could have happened." She sniffed back a tear. "Who could have done this to him?"

"Did he have any enemies?" Mitch asked.

"No." Myrna shook her head. "We have consistent five star reviews for our venue. Reginald makes sure that all the wedding parties are happy with our services, before and after their reception."

"You don't have any brides that were upset they couldn't get the date they wanted?" Lauren asked, thinking about Brianna. The girl had been insistent on Saturday, August fourteenth.

"Of course that happens at times," Myrna replied. "But Reginald knows how to temper their disappointment. He explains that they won't get a better experience anywhere else."

"Even the budget brides?" Zoe asked. "The price we were quoted didn't seem very budget to me."

"This place has a lot of running costs," Myrna answered. "Part of my job is doing the bookkeeping and paying the bills. And there are salaries for the three of us as well. Budget brides get a wonderful experience here, and they're not treated any differently to our VIP clients."

"Apart from the menu," Zoe muttered to Lauren.

"How many appointments did you have this morning?" Mitch asked.

"Just you, and Brianna, and her dad," Myrna replied.

Detective Castern strode down the hall.

"Myrna," he said. "Come with me."

Myrna looked like she wanted to gulp as she meekly followed him down the hall, passing Elizabeth on the way.

"How did you find Reginald?" Elizabeth joined them in the hallway. She dabbed her eyes with a white linen handkerchief. Apart from that, she looked competent and professional in her pastel blue suit.

Lauren quickly explained, glossing over the upsetting details.

"I don't know who could have killed him." Elizabeth shook her head.

"What did Detective Castern say when he took your statement?" Mitch probed.

"That I shouldn't talk to anyone else about it," she replied primly.

"That's true," he allowed.

"Even though Reggie told me you were a police detective." Elizabeth switched her gaze to Lauren. "Have you decided to take the Tuesday in October, dear?"

"No." Lauren and Mitch answered together. They glanced at each other and smiled briefly.

"Oh." Elizabeth sounded disappointed. "Would you still like to be on my cancellation list?"

"No, thank you," Lauren replied for both of them. Perhaps it wasn't fair of her, but she didn't want to hold her reception here now.

Elizabeth glanced down at Annie, as if noticing her for the first time. "You do know cats aren't allowed in here, don't you? I'm afraid she won't be able to attend your reception, if you still want to hold it here."

"Brrp." Annie's lower lip protruded a little, as if she were pouting.

"Annie is my co-maid of honor," Lauren informed her. "She's a big part of the wedding."

"Yeah, Lauren and Mitch can't get married if Annie isn't there." She glanced at Lauren. "Can you?"

"No." Lauren shook her head. It wouldn't feel right.

"That's correct," Mitch confirmed.

"Brrt." *Thank you.* Annie sounded happier.

Detective Castern's interview with Myrna took a while.

Elizabeth departed to her office, saying she would have to break the news to Reginald's family and friends.

"Let's explore." Zoe's eyes sparkled.

"Brrt!"

"Where?" Lauren asked.

"Just down the hall." Zoe waved her hand along the cream painted corridor. "I wonder what's in the rooms down there?"

"Why not?" Mitch said. "I'll go with you."

They strolled down the hall, Lauren wondering if Detective Castern would appear at any moment and bark at them. She decided it was worth the risk.

Zoe opened a door and they peered inside. The room was a miniature of the main reception room where they'd had last week's meeting – the same cream ceiling with decorative flat moldings, and the walls with tasteful gold accents at the corners.

But somehow the space didn't seem overwhelming in its perfection.

"So cute!" Zoe gazed around. "If they'd shown us this room last week …"

"I know." Lauren nodded. The smaller size seemed more her and Mitch, but she could tell it wouldn't hold fifty-three guests – and each person on the list was important to both of them.

"Yeah, too small." Sometimes it seemed Zoe could read her thoughts. "And Elizabeth said cats aren't allowed."

"Brrp," Annie agreed sadly.

They ventured further down the hall, Annie leading the way.

She suddenly pounced on something red.

"What is it?" Lauren bent down and picked up the item from the beige carpet.

"It's a rose petal." Zoe peered over her shoulder.

She handed it to Mitch.

"I'll put it into evidence, just in case." He pulled a small plastic bag out of his pocket and latex gloves. "But it could be nothing. Maybe Elizabeth has flowers in her office."

"The big room we were in last week had a bouquet of roses," Lauren said thoughtfully.

"And there were roses in the knot garden this morning," Zoe added.

"Brrt!"

"Thank you for finding this." Lauren praised her fur baby.

"Yeah, it could be an important clue." Zoe winked at the feline.

"Next," Detective Castern barked from the other end of the hall.

"I'll go," Zoe volunteered.

"Okay." Lauren nodded.

"Denman, the boss said if you're finished here with your *fiancée*, you can return to the station." Detective Castern informed him.

"You don't want my statement?" Mitch asked.

"I don't think it's necessary." He turned on his heel, Zoe reluctantly following.

"I can stay here with you," Mitch told Lauren. "I don't care what he says. I don't take orders from him."

"It's okay." She squeezed his hands. "Annie and I will be fine."

He kissed her tenderly, then strode down the hall. "I'll call you later," he promised, before rounding the corner.

"As soon as we're finished here, we'll go home," Lauren told Annie.

"Brrt!"

CHAPTER 6

By the time they were allowed to leave the building, as directed by Detective Castern, all Lauren wanted to do was go home and lie on the sofa with Annie, and try and forget today had ever happened.

"Detective Castern has a nerve," Zoe grumbled as they walked to the car. "By the way he acted with me, you'd think I'd killed Reginald. He didn't seem interested when I told him how we met Brianna and her dad when we got here."

"That's exactly how he was with me," Lauren admitted. "I think it would make his day – maybe the rest of his year – if *we* killed Reginald." She shook her head, trying to clear the image of Reginald's dead body from her mind, the paramedics working on him. "Poor man."

"Maybe Myrna did it," Zoe mused. "Or Elizabeth."

Lauren drove along the highway for a few minutes, feeling thirsty – and hungry.

"Ooh, stop!" Zoe pointed to an exit. "I definitely need some ice cream therapy."

"Me too." Lauren veered onto the ramp.

"Brrt!"

Although Annie didn't have an ice cream sundae like Lauren and Zoe, she seemed to enjoy the bottled water poured into her travel bowl.

"I feel much better," Zoe declared, setting down her cup on the dashboard. "Now we can go to Mrs. Finch's house and tell her what happened."

"Is that okay with you, Annie?"

"Brrt!" *Yes!*

Lauren started the ignition and soon they pulled up outside their friend's home.

The sweet, cream Victorian house with its neat lawn and little garden of orange Californian poppies lifted Lauren's spirits.

Mrs. Finch was suitably shocked when they told her about that morning's events.

"Oh, no. Lauren, dear, where will you hold your reception now?"

"Definitely not there." She tried to hide a shudder. "I think Mitch will understand."

"Of course he will." Mrs. Finch nodded.

"Do you think Aunt Celia has a backup venue?" Zoe asked. "When are you going to tell her about what happened this morning?"

"When we get home," Lauren replied, wishing she didn't have to do so. "I don't want her finding out from someone else."

"Good point." Zoe nodded.

Mrs. Finch promised to visit the café the next day, saying she was looking forward to tasting the new carrot cupcake.

"We'll save you one," Zoe promised. "In case they sell out in a snap!" She clicked her fingers.

After they arrived home, Lauren sat on the sofa, Annie by her side, and made the phone call. Her mother was suitably shocked, then resigned to the fact that Lauren didn't want to hold her wedding at Stately Vue Hall.

"I understand," her mom told her, disappointment in her tone. "And I'm afraid I don't have a backup venue in mind. Would you like me to look for you?"

Lauren tactfully told her it might be best if she and Mitch tried to find one on their own.

"Of course," her mother replied, brightening when Lauren enthused about Zoe's wedding gift – the pottery mugs that would feature the wedding date and a picture of Annie in her co-maid of honor floral headband.

"That sounds *so* Zoe," her mother replied. "And a very thoughtful gift. I can't wait to see them."

Lauren ended the call on a good note, and smiled down at Annie. "Mom understands about what happened today," she told her softly. "Now we have to find a new reception venue."

"Brrt," Annie replied thoughtfully.

After she and Annie relaxed for a while, Lauren whipped up a batch of her new creation for tomorrow, in the café's commercial kitchen. Her mouth watered as she thought of the cupcakes coming out of the oven in the morning, well risen and golden orange-brown, with cream cheese frosting swirled around the plump tops.

She made a mental note to put some away for themselves, and to give one to Ed.

When she finished in the café, she headed back to the cottage. Zoe lay on the pink sofa, sketching Annie, who turned her head to the left as Zoe directed.

"For future mugs," her cousin told her.

Lauren smiled at her fur baby modelling like a professional.

"Did Mitch call you yet?" Zoe asked.

"No." Lauren shook her head. She'd had her phone in her pocket while in the café. "He must be busy."

“Maybe he’ll have some inside info for us – you – when he phones,” Zoe said. “I wonder who killed Reginald?”

“I guess it’s either Elizabeth, Myrna, Brianna the spoiled bride, or her dad George.” Lauren sank onto the old sofa, covered with a pink slip.

“Unless it was a random intruder, or another client no one knew about, except Reginald.” Zoe snapped her fingers. “Yeah, maybe he did it!”

“Who?”

“Someone who wanted a hush-hush super-secret appointment with Reginald, and no one else knew about it. Like a movie star, or a rock star, or a politician, or a—”

“But it sounded like Brianna and her dad had the appointment before ours,” Lauren pointed out. “How would another client have time to kill Reginald before we got there?”

“Someone did.”

“Brrt!”

“Maybe it was only a five-minute appointment,” Zoe mused. “And he met Reginald in the garden, so no one would see him. And he got mad about something and BAM! He killed Reginald."

"But why?"

"That's what we have to find out." Zoe's eyes sparkled with the allure of sleuthing.

"You mean that's what Mitch has to find out – although I guess it will be Detective Castern this time."

"Yuck!"

"Brrt!"

Unfortunately, Detective Castern did not seem to be a fan of Annie's, although she'd been friendly to him in the past.

"I think we have enough to do at the moment without investigating," Lauren said. "I have to find a new venue—"

"I'll help you."

"Brrt!" *Yes!*

"Thanks." She smiled at both of them. "I still need to decide on the invitations, and start thinking about flowers, and then there's dress shopping ..." she trailed off.

"We'll help you with those too," Zoe declared. "I've already researched cat safe flowers and there are plenty of varieties you can use in your bouquet and we can wear in our headbands, like orchids, roses, and snapdragons."

"That sounds great."

"Brrt!" Annie trotted over to Lauren and jumped in her lap.

"We'd better go to Sacramento to find a dress," Zoe advised. "I've been watching some of those wedding dress TV shows, and sometimes it takes the bride a *long* time to find the gown she loves." She noticed the panicked look on Lauren's face. "Oops – sorry."

"It's okay." She'd been wondering how easy it would be to find a dress she wanted to wear down the aisle. Mitch said he loved her curves, but she wanted to wear something she adored and made her look good.

"And then there's hair and make-up." Lauren sank back against the sofa cushions. "Maybe Mitch had the right idea about eloping."

"Really?" Zoe's eyes widened.

“No.” Lauren drew in a breath. “Not really.” She was sure that her parents, and all their friends and family would be disappointed if she and Mitch *did* elope. And she didn’t think she could get married without Annie being there.

“Oh, good.” Zoe sounded relieved. “Because if you did run off together, I’m sure Aunt Celia would blame me for not stopping you, considering I’m co-maid of honor.”

“Brrt!”

CHAPTER 7

Lauren hummed as she swirled cream cheese frosting on top of the carrot cupcakes the next morning. Mitch had called yesterday afternoon, agreeing with her that they shouldn't have the reception at Stately Vue Hall.

The preliminary medical reports indicated that Reginald had been hit on the head before being shoved into the hedge, with flowers stuffed into his nose and mouth, including petals similar to the one Annie found inside the venue. The head wound explained the trickle of blood Zoe had spied down his cheek.

Lauren shivered at the thought, and made herself think about more pleasant things. Like her customers hopefully raving about her new creation.

"Ed, tell me what you think." She offered him a cupcake. With monster rolling pins for arms, and short but shaggy auburn hair, Ed made pastry like a dream. Although Lauren loved making cakes, she was the first to admit her pastry wasn't as good as Ed's.

"Thanks." He smiled briefly. "Let me know if there's anything I can do to help with the wedding."

"You're invited," she replied instantly, realizing she'd forgotten to tell him before now.

Lauren had already told him they'd found Reginald's body, and he'd been suitably shocked.

"Would you like a plus one?" she asked, knowing he was dating a fellow volunteer at the local animal shelter.

"That would be great." His white teeth gleamed briefly. "I can invite Rebecca."

She'd better amend the guest list to fifty-four.

"As soon as Mitch and I find a place, we'll send out the invitations."

"Sure." He nodded.

Lauren carried the tray of goodies out to the café and slid them behind the glass case.

"Did you keep some for us?" Zoe eyed the treats.

"Yes."

"Good."

A couple of minutes later, she unlocked the glass and oak entrance door. She'd also made lavender, and lemon poppyseed cupcakes, and Ed had already baked a batch of his popular honeyed walnut pastries, and was currently working on apricot Danishes. Now all they needed were customers.

Lauren wasn't disappointed.

Mrs. Finch was their first arrival, wearing a beige skirt and pastel pink blouse.

"Hello, dears." She stood at the *Please Wait to be Seated* sign.

"Brrt!" Annie ran to greet her, and slowly led her to a small table near the counter.

Mrs. Finch tapped her way there with her walking stick.

"You're just in time to try the carrot cakes," Zoe declared. "Fresh out of the oven."

"I can't wait." Mrs. Finch beamed. "And I would love a latte as well, please, dear."

"Coming right up." Zoe zoomed back to the counter.

Lauren heard the exchange and was already grinding the beans, the machine growling away.

She waved to Mrs. Finch. Annie chatted away to her in a series of brrts and chirps.

Lauren finished off the latte with a peacock design. She and Zoe had taken an advanced latte art class a while ago, and it had really paid off.

"Thank you, Lauren, dear." Mrs. Finch picked up the cup with a wobbly hand. "I do love your peacocks. And swans."

"Thanks." Lauren smiled.

Zoe placed the cupcake in front of her. "Tell us what you think. Lauren and I love these new carrot cakes."

"I'm sure I will, too." Mrs. Finch gazed at the creation, admiring the decorative frosting swirl. “I think you might have outdone yourself this time, Lauren.”

“I hope so.” She loved giving her customers and friends delicious treats as well as amazing coffee.

“Have you thought about making your wedding cake yourself?” Mrs. Finch inquired, forking up a small mouthful.

Panic fluttered in her stomach. “Not really.”

“Ooh, you should!” Zoe’s eyes rounded. “Why not? I bet your cake will taste just as good as any specialist baker’s.”

“Thanks.” Lauren touched her cousin’s arm. “But what about all the decorating? I can do frosting swirls, but what about all the specialized flowers and rosettes? I could manage some of it but probably not all of it.”

“That’s a point.” Zoe tapped her cheek. “And I guess you really don’t have time to take a class, with all the other five-hundred things you need to do before you marry Mitch. Hmm.”

“I’m sorry I brought it up.” Mrs. Finch looked regretful.

“It’s okay,” Lauren assured her. “I’ll just have to add organizing a wedding cake on my list now.”

“Maybe we should have three to-do lists,” Zoe suggested. “An immediate one, then one with a two-to-three-week timeline, and one called, things we don’t need to do until the last minute.”

“Zoe might have a point.” Mrs. Finch chuckled.

“Or—” Zoe paused dramatically. “You could make wedding cupcakes – with a cupcake tower! And have different flavors, so guests could choose their favorites. And I’d bet it would be a lot cheaper than getting a fancy baker to make you something.” She turned to Mrs. Finch. “The posh reception venue quoted us three-hundred-and-fifty dollars for a single tiered wedding cake.”

“That *is* a lot of money.” Mrs. Finch looked shocked.

“Especially with everything else Lauren has to pay for.” Zoe nodded.

"You mean my parents," Lauren said.

"Yeah, Aunt Celia is paying for all the bride stuff."

"And my dad," Lauren reminded her.

"Oh, that's right." She giggled. "Your dad's nice. So's Aunt Celia."

"Thanks."

"I'm glad your parents are able to give you a lovely wedding." Mrs. Finch beamed at Lauren. "And this carrot cake is delicious, dear. When I get home I'll call all my friends and tell them about it."

"Thanks, Mrs. Finch!" Zoe grinned.

"Now, do you have an update on the poor man who was killed at the reception venue?" she asked.

Lauren related what Mitch had told her over the phone.

Mrs. Finch tsked. "Someone must have quite a temper on them, to kill him in that way."

"Yeah, especially stuffing the flowers into his mouth," Zoe added. "He – or she – really wanted to make sure Reginald was dead. He even had some in his nose!"

Mrs. Finch shook her head in dismay.

A few more customers came in, and after Annie greeted them and led them to their tables, she returned to Mrs. Finch.

A short while later, Lauren smiled at the balding Episcopalian priest. "Hi, Father Mike." Of medium height and build, he was beloved by the whole town.

"Brrt!" Annie trotted up to him.

"Hi, Lauren, and Zoe." He beamed at both of them. "Have you decided where to hold your reception?"

"Not yet." She quickly told him about the murder.

"That's terrible." Concern flickered across his face. "I didn't know the poor man, but I'll pray for him."

"Thanks, Father," Lauren replied.

"How's Mrs. Snuggle?" Zoe asked. They'd recently cat sat the white Persian when Father Mike had visited Florida for a church conference. He'd adopted the Queen and show cat when her owner had been murdered, since it had been difficult to find her a new home due to her grumpy demeanor.

"Ever since I returned from Miami, she's been a lot more affectionate," he marveled. "She sits on my lap most nights and loves watching that movie over and over about the princess who discovers her whole life is a lie, apart from being a princess."

"I love that movie, too." Zoe grinned.

"Brrt!"

"Maybe she realized when she stayed with us how much she really does like you," Lauren commented.

Mrs. Snuggle's new life with Father Mike was totally different to her former one. Now she could relax all day and not be on display at a cat show, or nursing another litter of kittens. When the priest adopted her, he'd had her spayed, and had been kind and gentle with her, even when she remained grumpy and unaffectionate.

Lauren suspected that Mrs. Snuggle finally realized what a good home she had with Father Mike, and that he loved her.

"Maybe she and Annie can have a play date one day," Zoe suggested.

Annie looked interested at the suggestion. She had done her best to look after the Persian, taking her cat sitting duties seriously, but although they had played together briefly, Mrs. Snuggle had spent most of her time with the trio watching TV and moping.

"Mrs. Snuggle might like that." Father Mike smiled. "I'll check with her."

"Okay." Lauren nodded.

"Let me know when your wedding is, and I'll officiate," Father Mike told her. "I'm looking forward to it."

"Thank you." Lauren smiled. "Mitch and I can't think of anyone else we'd rather have marry us."

They took his order of a latte and carrot cupcake.

Annie led him to Mrs. Finch's table, the senior beaming in delight when he joined her.

"Two of Annie's favorite people together." Zoe grinned as she glanced at them.

A short while later, more customers trickled in.

"Where's my cutie pie?" Martha barreled into the café, pushing her rolling walker at an impressive speed. She had curly gray hair, and wore blue pedal pushers and a matching t-shirt.

"Brrt!" *Here!* Annie scampered over, and leaped onto the black padded vinyl seat of the walker.

"Hi, Martha," Lauren greeted her.

"You have to tell me all about the murdered man," Martha instructed.

"How do you know about him?" Zoe's eyes widened.

"I got the lowdown this morning from the senior center."

"That place is a hotbed of gossip."

"You know it." Martha nodded.

"You've got to try Lauren's new cupcakes," Zoe informed her.

"They do look good." Martha eyed the treats behind the glass case.

"What would you like to drink?" Lauren asked.

"Hmm." Martha wrinkled her nose. "You know I love my hot chocolate, even in summer, especially with those yummy marshmallows you put in it, but right now I feel like I need a little pick me up as well."

"Ooh – what about a latte with marshmallows?" Zoe's eyes sparkled.

Martha's mouth parted. "Now you're talking!"

Lauren furrowed her brow. "I haven't made a marshmallow latte before. If you don't enjoy it, I'll make you whatever you like instead."

"I'm sure I'll *love* it," Martha replied.

"Yeah, what's not to like about coffee and marshmallows?" Zoe grinned.

"You haven't tried the two together, have you?" Lauren asked.

"No," Zoe admitted after a second.

Annie directed Martha to a table with a series of brrts from her position on the walker. They finally stopped at a four-seater in the middle of the room.

Annie jumped from the walker to one of the chairs, while Martha sat opposite her.

Lauren steamed the milk for a large latte, while Zoe grabbed the jar of marshmallows.

"I can't wait to see how this turns out. I might make one for myself during my break."

"Good idea," Lauren replied. "I might try it as well."

After making the latte, she added a generous amount of mini marshmallows, and stirred it carefully, not wanting to splash the hot liquid.

"That looks awesome!" The latte was pale fawn with pink and white streaks from the marshmallows.

"Let's hope it tastes awesome."

She carried it over to Martha, Zoe following with the cupcake.

"Well?" Zoe asked impatiently a second later after Martha took a sip. "How is it?"

"Yummy!" Martha grinned.

"We can call it Martha's marshmallow latte," Zoe suggested.

"Really?" Martha's eyes lit up.

"If you don't mind," Lauren said.

"Why would I mind? I'll be famous – in here at least."

"You mean you aren't already?" Zoe giggled.

Martha and Lauren joined in the laughter, Annie adding a happy, "Brrt."

"I'm going to write this up on the chalkboard." Zoe had recently bought a mini board but they hadn't used it yet. She dug it out of the drawer and advertised the new beverage on it.

"How much should we ask for it?" she asked Lauren.

"We'll charge Martha the normal latte price," she decided, "since it was her suggestion, but we should add a little extra to cover the cost of the marshmallows when we make it for other customers."

"What about thirty cents?" Zoe suggested.

Lauren eyed the jar of mini marshmallows. "That sounds about right, if we put in a large spoonful each time, like we did with Martha's."

Zoe wrote up the new drink, and set up the chalkboard on the counter. “I hope we don’t run out of marshmallows.”

When Martha paid her bill, she enthused about the new beverage. “I’m going to tell everyone down at the senior center.”

“Awesome.” Zoe waved at the chalkboard. “Look!”

“I really *am* going to be famous.” She grinned.

When Lauren handed back her change, she asked, “How’s the wedding planning going?”

They quickly filled her in about their new search for a venue.

“And the invitations?” Martha asked hopefully. “Have they gone out yet?”

“Not yet, but you’re invited.” Lauren smiled.

“Goody!”

A few of their customers tried the new latte, pleased expressions on their faces afterward.

“Maybe we’ll need to buy some more marshmallows,” Zoe observed that afternoon. The level in the jar was now dangerously low.

"I've got more in the pantry," Lauren replied. "But you're right. If Martha tells everyone at the senior center about her new drink, we might be slammed tomorrow!"

CHAPTER 8

Lauren's prediction became true the next morning. Martha's marshmallow latte was a hit. So were the carrot cupcakes. Lauren baked more, since they had sold out the previous day.

Ms. Tobin came in, requesting the new drink – and cupcake.

"Everyone has been telling me about Martha's beverage this morning," she said. "And also that she's been invited to your wedding."

"So are you," Lauren replied quickly with a smile. It was true.

"Brrt!" Annie added.

"Oh." Pleasure flickered over Ms. Tobin's face. "That is very kind of you, Lauren. Do you have a gift registry?"

Lauren's eyes widened. "No."

"Let me write that on my list." Zoe whipped out her phone from her capris pocket. "I'm co-maid of honor."

"And who is the other maid of honor?"

"Brrt!" *Me!*

Ms. Tobin smiled down at the silver-gray tabby as they both stood at the counter. "I should have guessed, Annie."

She ordered a large marshmallow latte a little dubiously and a carrot cake.

"You're going to love both of them," Zoe promised her, as Annie whisked her off to a small table near the counter.

"I hope," Lauren murmured.

Annie chatted to Ms. Tobin while Lauren made the coffee and Zoe plated the cupcake.

"Everyone is loving the carrot," Zoe told her. "Ed told me this morning how good it is."

"He told me, too." Lauren smiled. Ed didn't give praise lightly.

She'd also made super vanilla, and Norwegian apple cupcakes that morning, but her new creation was outselling both.

When Ms. Tobin approached the register to pay, there was a smile on her face.

"I must admit, Lauren, I was a bit doubtful about your new marshmallow latte, but I actually enjoyed it."

"Awesome." Zoe grinned.

"I'm glad," Lauren replied.

"I might get it next time, but perhaps you could put in a few less marshmallows for me? I did find it a tad sweet."

"Of course," Lauren promised, making a mental note to remember.

"Do let me know about your gift registry." Ms. Tobin waved goodbye to them.

After a quick lunch for both of them, Zoe taking hers first, and then Lauren with Annie, there was a lull.

"I'm definitely going to make myself something." Zoe's eyes lit up as she scooped a lot of marshmallows into her large latte.

"OMG." She closed her eyes for a second.

"I think you have more marshmallows in there than Martha," Lauren teased.

"Yep." Zoe did not sound apologetic.

"Ooh – I'm going to add something to the chalkboard." Zoe put down her mug and wrote neatly on the black surface, the chalk making a slight squeak as she did so.

"There!" She turned the board around so Lauren could read it.

"This has Zoe's seal of approval." Lauren stifled a giggle.

"Maybe you should add, "and Martha's."

"Good idea." Zoe added, "*Martha loves this!"* "This should bring in more customers."

That afternoon, Annie took a well-deserved rest in her pink cat basket, and Lauren and Zoe sat on the stools behind the counter for a while.

The few patrons chatted, ate and drank, a low hum of conversation providing pleasant background noise.

"Hi, Lauren." Brooke, the local hairdresser, entered. Her chestnut locks had attractive reddish highlights, cut in a long bob with feathered ends. The hair color flattered her friendly green eyes. Her short-sleeved green top with beige pants looked cool and comfortable.

"Hi, Brooke." Lauren jumped off the stool.

"Brrt!" Annie woke up from her doze and ambled over to her.

"You've got to try our new drink, and Lauren's new creation." Zoe's eyes sparkled.

Brooke glanced at the chalkboard. "That sounds cute."

"It even has Ms. Tobin's seal of approval," Zoe told her. "Hmm, maybe I should add that as well."

"Will you have room?" Lauren asked. "And remember, Ms. Tobin asked for a few less marshmallows next time."

"That's true." Zoe tapped her cheek.

"I will definitely try your new latte," Brooke said. "And your carrot cupcakes. Some of my clients told me about them this morning in the salon."

"Really?" Lauren smiled.

"Uh-huh." Brooke nodded. "And they also spoke about your upcoming wedding. And how the man was murdered at the venue you were considering."

"Wow." Zoe eyed their friend. "You might know more gossip than Martha."

"You know that ladies getting their hair done like to talk to their stylist." Brooke smiled. "I haven't told you anything that's not common knowledge."

"That's true," Lauren replied.

"Brrt!"

"I'd be honored if you would allow me to do your hair for the wedding, Lauren," Brooke said earnestly. "It could be my wedding gift to you."

"Oh." She blinked back sudden tears. "I'd love that. Thank you. You and Jeff are invited as guests. You're on the list."

"At this rate, we won't need to send out invitations," Zoe joked. "Because we'll have told everyone in person!"

She and Zoe had met the stylist when Zoe had trimmed Lauren's hair – with slightly disastrous results. Brooke had just set up her salon in Gold Leaf Valley, and had quickly made Lauren's locks presentable again.

"We should book you for the whole wedding party." Zoe dug out her phone from her pocket. "Then I can cross that off my list."

"You have hair on your list?" Lauren peered at the screen.

"Not yet," her cousin admitted, "but I will in a sec." Her thumbs got to work on the digital keyboard.

"I think Zoe's right," Lauren said. "Are you available to take care of everyone in the wedding party? For your usual wedding fees, of course."

Brooke's face lit up. "How about I do your and Zoe's hair as my gift, and give you a ten percent discount off my usual rates for everyone else?"

"That's very kind of you." Lauren smiled.

"My pleasure." Brooke winked. "It looks like I was right about you and

Mitch being the next ones down the aisle."

"How's your wedding coming along?" Zoe put her phone back in her pocket.

"Jeff and I have booked our venue," she told them, "but it's in a few months' time."

"You're not getting married at Stately Vue Hall?" Zoe's eyes widened.

"No." Brooke shook her head. "We had a meeting there, and I loved the knot garden, but I didn't think it was quite me and Jeff."

Lauren nodded, knowing what she meant.

Lauren made the special latte, while Zoe plated the cupcake. Annie had whisked Brooke off to a four-seater near the counter.

When they took over the order, Brooke invited them to sit with her.

"Thanks." Lauren sank down in the pine chair. "We had a busy morning."

"And you got one of the last carrots." Zoe pointed to her plate.

"I can't wait to try it."

All three of them seemed to hold their breath as Brooke forked up a mouthful.

Bliss exploded across her face.

"This is wonderful, Lauren."

"Thanks." She couldn't contain her smile.

They compared notes with Brooke about their upcoming ceremonies. Their friend recommended a dress shop in Sacramento where she'd found the perfect wedding dress. Zoe noted down the address.

More customers trickled in, and Lauren and Zoe regretfully rose. After Annie seated the newcomers, she returned to Brooke, talking to her in a series of brrts. Lauren wondered if her fur baby was telling their friend that she was co-maid of honor with Zoe.

CHAPTER 9

The next evening, Mitch and Lauren went out to dinner.

Mitch drove them to one of their favorite restaurants, a bistro on the edge of town. Although it was still daylight, the outside fairy lights had been turned on, giving it a magical touch.

"I just love it here." Lauren sighed as they sat down at a small table in the corner. The interior was rustic but elegant, and served some of her favorite food, including the desserts.

"I know." Mitch captured her hand across the white tablecloth. Tonight, he wore a white dress shirt and charcoal slacks. He gazed at her. "I feel like I haven't seen you for a long time, when in reality it's only been two days."

"Is Detective Castern close to catching the killer?"

"No." His mouth firmed. "He's interviewed Brianna, the spoiled girl who wanted to have her wedding there, and her father, but they lawyered up."

"Both of them?" Lauren's eyes widened.

"Yeah. Apparently, Brianna's dad is a big deal in real estate, and has lawyers on speed dial. Although Detective Castern wanted to ask them routine questions from what I know, they refused to answer."

"And he let them get away with that?"

Mitch shrugged. "For now. He doesn't think they're guilty, and he's focusing his efforts on Elizabeth and Myrna."

"Myrna did find Reginald," Lauren mused.

"Yeah, and sometimes it's the person who finds the victim who *is* guilty," Mitch said. "And since Castern has gone in hard for the wrong person before, I think he's taking a less aggressive approach this time in regard to Brianna and her dad George."

"Hmm." She wished Mitch was on the case instead of Detective Castern.

"So, what are you up to at work, if you're not on this case?" she asked.

"Missing equipment from the croquet club."

"Do people still play it these days?"

"Apparently it's popular with the senior set. And the mallets can cost hundreds of dollars each."

"Wow." She hadn't realized. "We're going to have find a new reception venue," she reminded him.

"I know." He nodded.

"Is Chris getting organized with lists like Zoe is?"

"He's starting to." He chuckled. "He called me last night asking about tuxedos, or if I had any idea what I wanted us to wear for the ceremony. I told him I'd go with something traditional. But no ruffled shirts or blue tuxes."

She couldn't imagine Mitch wearing something like that.

"What about you? Have you gone dress shopping yet?"

"No, but Brooke recommended a store in Sacramento, so Zoe and I will take a look when we have a free day."

"Good." He lifted her hand to his lips.

A man dressed in brown slacks and a cream shirt came over to them.

"Mitch, Lauren, I wanted to let you know that we've just started opening for weekend lunches."

"Really, Joe?" Lauren gazed around the half-full restaurant. "That's great."

"I'm making the rounds, telling all our customers. From noon to three, Saturdays and Sundays."

Lauren relaxed against the comfortable chair. She gazed at the tasteful lighting and the way the staff and Joe, the owner, had always made them feel welcome. And the food was always delicious.

She caught Mitch's eye.

"Are you thinking what I'm thinking?" he asked her.

"I think so." She smiled.

"Do you hold wedding receptions?" they asked at the same time.

***

After going over the details with Joe, they settled on a date in two months' time, on a Saturday.

"I've had to add a plus one to Ed's invitation," she said. "I'm not sure if there'll be any others."

"He's bringing Rebecca?" Mitch asked.

"Yes."

"It shouldn't be a problem," Joe told them. He glanced around the large room. "Just let us know for sure two weeks before the day so we can order enough food for everyone. We should have enough tables and chairs."

"Thank you." Lauren smiled at him gratefully. "We have fifty-four on the guest list at the moment."

"I've been thinking about hiring this place out for receptions and doing the catering," he confided to them. "But I haven't really gone over the costs for the food or beverages yet."

Lauren and Mitch told them the price they had been quoted for the budget bride menu at Stately Vue Hall, and Joe looked shocked.

"I can do a lot better than that for the same amount of money," he replied. "And I won't charge you a venue fee either, since you're regulars. I can also provide a licensed bartender at cost."

"It all sounds wonderful." Lauren blinked back sudden tears. She must have been a lot more stressed about the preparations than she'd thought.

"Most of the guests are local, so coming here will be a lot easier for them than Stately Vue Hall." Mitch spoke.

"And I'm sure the guests from Sacramento won't mind travelling down here," Lauren added.

"I think my folks will be thrilled that we've finally found somewhere we're happy with."

"Why don't I put something together and email it to you?" Joe suggested. "You'll get it by tomorrow lunchtime."

"That would be wonderful." Lauren smiled.

"Thanks." Mitch nodded to him in a man-to-man way.

They settled on tonight's entrees. Lauren chose one of her favorites - pork with four varieties of apples and Mitch opted for steak with mushroom sauce.

"Oh." Lauren put down her fork. "I forgot about Annie! I didn't ask Joe if she'd be welcome here."

"Are you sure the noise and so many guests won't be a problem for her?" There was concern in Mitch's voice. "I know she's used to the café and dealing with the customers there, even when you're slammed, but …"

"You're right." Lauren nodded. "And she's going to be part of the ceremony. But I don't want her to feel left out at the reception. I was thinking, maybe she could come here for a few minutes and take it all in, and then if it gets too much for her, I can drive her home."

"You mean *we'll* take her home." He looked at her tenderly.

"Thank you." This time, she caught his hand across the table.

***

The next day, Lauren checked her phone.

"Look." She nudged Zoe. The café wasn't busy at the moment, although it was before the lunch rush. "I've received an email from Joe with sample menus and pricing."

Zoe peered over her shoulder. "It sounds yummy. Much better than pasta with tomato sauce at Stately Vue Hall."

"Yes."

"I like the sound of this one. Mini crab cakes with micro-greens, steak or Tuscan chicken, and chocolate mousse or lemon cheesecake. Thirty-five dollars per head. Are you seeing Mitch today?" Zoe asked. "You could show him."

"He said he'd try to stop by."

"Annie!" A small child with blonde curls tugged at her mother's hand as they entered the café.

"Brrt!" Annie scampered over from her cat basket.

"Hi, Molly. Hi, Claire." Lauren greeted their friends.

"Hi." Claire, a tall athletic woman, smiled at them.

"I'm going to big school soon," Molly informed them importantly.

"That's exciting." Zoe winked at her. "I'm sure you'll love it."

"That's what Mommy said." Molly turned her face up to Claire and beamed.

"How's your Kitty?" Lauren asked.

They'd hosted a cat adoption event several months ago, and Molly had fallen in love with a kitten who looked a lot like Annie.

"She's getting big." Molly giggled. "Like me."

"Here are the latest photos." Claire pulled out her phone from her lightweight pants' pocket and showed them – Molly, Kitty, and a ball, Molly and Kitty watching TV together, Molly lying on the floor and Kitty pouncing on her stomach. The joy on Molly's face in that photo was priceless.

They admired the photos. Claire crouched and showed Annie as well.

"Brrt." There was a pleased look on Annie's face when she looked at the images.

"I must try one of your new carrot cakes," Claire said. She glanced toward the glass case. "Do you have any today?"

"Yes," Lauren assured her.

"You'll love it." Zoe grinned.

"And a marshmallow latte, please."

"How did you know about that?" Lauren asked.

"I bumped into a friend yesterday at the grocery store who raved about it."

"It was Martha's idea," Zoe said.

"Would you like a babycino, Molly?" Lauren asked the little girl.

"Yes!" Molly grinned. "Pwease," she added.

Annie showed them to a large table in the middle of the room.

Lauren and Zoe brought their orders over to them.

"How is the wedding planning going?" Claire inquired.

"You're invited," Zoe said instantly.

"Yes." Lauren glanced at her cousin. "Now that we have a date, I can send out the invitations. Oh, and check with Father Mike that he can marry us on that Saturday."

Zoe dug out her phone, her thumbs busy. "Got it."

Claire looked amused, while Molly stroked Annie who sat on the chair next to her, with gentle "fairy pats".

"Do you have a gift registry?" Claire asked.

"Not yet." Lauren glanced at Zoe.

"It's on my list." Zoe peered at her phone.

Claire tried the carrot cupcake, smiling after the first bite. "It's wonderful, Lauren." She looked at the frothy beverage. "And I can't wait to try this latte." She took a sip. "It does have an unusual flavor, but—" she took another sip "—there's just something about it."

"Molly have?" The little girl looked hopefully at her mother's plate.

"Here." Claire broke off a decent sized piece of cake and put it on the extra plate Lauren had provided.

"Yum!" Molly smacked her lips together, a smear of cream cheese frosting just below her nose. "Molly have more?"

Claire gave her another piece of the cupcake, then looked down at her plate. There wasn't much left.

"I think I'd better get one of these cupcakes to go when I pay," she said ruefully.

"Of course." Lauren smiled.

Molly slurped her babycino, a small concoction of frothed milk, mini marshmallows, and a dusting of chocolate powder. When she'd finished, she had a little smear of melted marshmallow alongside the cream cheese frosting on her upper lip.

"Cino!" She sighed in satisfaction.

Claire pulled out a tissue and wiped her daughter's face, smiling as she did so.

They chatted with Claire and Molly for a few minutes, giving them more details about the wedding.

"Lauren getting married?" Molly's blue eyes rounded. "Pwincess!" She pointed to Lauren.

"That would be nice." Lauren blushed a little.

"Of course you'll look like a princess," Zoe assured her.

"Molly's been watching cartoons about princesses," Claire told them.

"Wait until you see me and Annie." Zoe giggled. "We're co-maids of honor, and we're going to wear matching floral headbands."

"Oooh!" Molly's expression was one of wonder.

CHAPTER 10

Mitch entered the café that afternoon, just after the lunch rush.

"Hi." He leaned over the counter and kissed her.

"Hi." She smiled.

"Why don't you two sit down?" Zoe flapped a hand at them. "I can handle everything here."

"Brrt!" Annie agreed, suddenly appearing. She stood next to Mitch.

"Thanks." Lauren smiled at her cousin gratefully.

They followed Annie to a four-seater at the rear. Annie hopped up on the chair next to Lauren's, and bunted her hand. She obliged by stroking her velvety soft fur.

"Now we have a reception venue and a firm date, we need to check in with Father Mike," she began.

"Let's do it right now." He dug out his phone.

After a couple of minutes talking to the priest, he ended the call. Lauren was already smiling – from hearing Mitch's side of the conversation, there didn't seem to be a problem.

"All set," he told her.

"Good. Now we can send out the invitations – except people have already asked me if we have a gift registry."

"I'll let you handle that," he replied. "I wouldn't have a clue."

"Okay. We need to include the gift registry details on the invitations. But I was thinking – we pretty much have everything we need, don't we? You'll be moving into the cottage with me, and I can't really think of anything I'd like or need. How about you?"

He thought for a moment. "No, not really."

"So, what about giving our guests a choice? I can set up a gift registry, but if our friends and family would rather make a donation, I thought we could nominate the local animal shelter where Ed volunteers. They're always in need of funds."

His dark brown eyes crinkled at the corners.

"Just another reason why I love you." His voice was soft. "I think it's a great idea." He paused. "What about Zoe?"

"What about her?" Her brow crinkled.

"Have you two spoken about what's going to happen after we get married?"

"No." Her eyes widened. If she'd thought about it, she'd had the vague notion that Zoe would probably live in the cottage with them, and continue to date Chris.

"It's okay if she wants to live with us," he assured her.

"Brrt!" Annie agreed.

"I guess Zoe and I have to do some thinking," Lauren said slowly.

Zoe was a big part of her life, and they'd been roomies for a few years now. She knew they'd still work together at the café, but if her cousin moved out, things would be different. She told herself that her life was changing anyway, with her upcoming marriage.

She showed Mitch the sample menus from the bistro. He was in agreement with choosing the thirty-five dollars per head menu.

"I'll confirm it now." She typed out a reply and hit send on her phone.

"Do you have any more news about the murder?" she asked.

"No." His mouth twisted. "Detective Castern is being very close mouthed in the office. All I know is that he still likes either Elizabeth or Myrna."

"Do you think Elizabeth was faking her grief on Monday?" Lauren frowned. Had Reginald's ex-wife actually shown much grief?

"People react in different ways," Mitch replied. "And they were divorced. She might have felt relieved after the first shock, because now she doesn't have to work with him. But that wouldn't happen to us." He reached for her hand. "Getting divorced."

"I hope not," Lauren replied with feeling.

After a short while, Mitch left, grabbing a latte to go and a super vanilla cupcake, which was still his favorite, although the carrot was a close second.

How was she going to have the difficult conversation with Zoe about living arrangements after the wedding?

Just as she was about to broach the subject, one of their favorite customers – and friends – came in.

"Hi, Hans." Zoe beamed at him.

"Hello, Zoe, and Lauren." The dapper man in his sixties, with a slight trace of a German accent, greeted them.

"Brrt!" Annie trotted up to him as he stood at the *Please Wait to be Seated* sign.

"Hello, *Liebchen*." He smiled down at the silver-gray tabby.

"Brrt!" *Follow me.* Annie slowly led the way, as if she knew he couldn't walk very fast, to a small table near the counter.

"What would you like?" Lauren and Zoe approached the duo.

"I will have my usual cappuccino, please," Hans requested. "I have heard of your marshmallow latte, but I think it might be a little sweet for me. And one of your new carrot cakes, if you have any."

"One of the last few." Zoe winked at him.

He inquired about the wedding planning, and Zoe invited him before Lauren could get the chance.

"We'll be sending out the invitations very soon," Lauren added. "We're having the reception at the bistro on the edge of town."

"Ach." He nodded. "I have heard the food is very good there."

"It is." Lauren smiled. "Mitch and I go there a lot."

"Yeah, Chris and I have been a few times and we haven't been disappointed," Zoe added.

Annie chatted to Hans in a series of brrts and chirps, while Lauren and Zoe took care of the order.

They brought over the cappuccino and cupcake, Hans praising both. "You make the best coffee, Lauren, and now I know why everyone at the senior center is talking about this carrot cake." He pointed to the treat, piled high with cream cheese frosting. "It looks wonderful."

"Thank you," Lauren replied, wondering if the reaction she'd gotten to her new creation was because she hadn't come up with a fresh idea for a couple of months.

They chatted to Hans for a few minutes, then had to attend to new customers. Annie greeted and seated them, before returning to Hans, one of her favorite people.

When all the orders had been taken care of, Lauren turned to Zoe.

"Can we talk for a minute?"

"Sure." Zoe looked at her quizzically. "What's up?"

Lauren took a deep breath.

"I was just thinking, what's going to happen to our living arrangements after the wedding? Mitch and I are happy to have you as a roomie, but we haven't talked about what *you* would like to do."

"Well, I was thinking I could take over Mitch's lease on his apartment. I don't want to cramp your style." Zoe winked. "You can invite me over for dinner – a lot – and we can still have our double dates with the guys, and chili night at Chris's. We'll see each other every day – well, five or six days per week, if we're still going to visit Mrs. Finch on Mondays."

"Of course we are," Lauren replied. "And craft club on Friday nights."

"Good." Zoe nodded. "That's settled."

"I don't want you to think we're pushing you out of the cottage – your home." Lauren touched her cousin's arm.

"You're not." Zoe shook her head. "But you guys will be *married.* You don't want me hanging around like a third wheel, and I don't think I want to do that, either. The wedding is going to change some things but we'll still be besties – and cousins – forever."

"You know we will," Lauren replied fiercely, blinking back tears.

After taking a deep breath, and giving Zoe a slightly watery smile, she said, "We need to decide on a gift registry. Mitch has left that up to me."

"Guys." Zoe flapped a hand. "No problem. We can talk about it tonight. There's that nice department store in Sacramento we could visit – ooh, and while we're there, we can check out that bridal shop Brooke recommended."

"Great idea." Lauren smiled. "I'm so glad you're my maid of honor."

"*Co-maid* of honor." Zoe grinned.

***

That evening, Lauren, Annie, and Zoe discussed their plans for the upcoming weekend.

"We can hit Sacramento Saturday afternoon and check out the department store and bridal shop. On Sunday, I'll go to the pottery studio and work on the mugs. Now I have a date for the wedding, I can really get started on them." Zoe beamed.

"And tomorrow night, we have craft club with Mrs. Finch." Lauren sounded guilty. "I haven't made any progress on your scarf all week."

"No worries. As long as I get it for Christmas."

"Brrt!"

"And on Monday we'll do our normal grocery shopping and visit Mrs. Finch," Lauren added.

"Definitely." Zoe nodded. "I might have to go back to the pottery studio in the afternoon, though. It depends how much I can get done on Sunday."

"What about Chris?" Lauren furrowed her brow. "Has he been working extra shifts lately?"

"Yeah." Zoe's tone turned glum. "That's why I've been staying at home more in the evening. Plus, Annie and I have been busy with our wedding duties." She winked at the cat.

"Brrt!" Annie shut one eye in a definite wink back to Zoe.

"What's been happening with the murder investigation?" Zoe's voice grew serious. "You haven't mentioned it much."

"That's because there's not much to mention," Lauren replied. "Detective Castern is still on the case and is apparently keeping his opinions close to his chest this time. Apart from thinking it's either Elizabeth or Myrna."

"Honestly." Zoe shook her head. "It's been, what? A week now? And he still hasn't caught the killer? And what's Mitch doing?"

"Discovering who's stealing equipment from the croquet club."

"Hmm." Zoe tapped her cheek. "If the police can't catch the murderer, we might have to."

"Zoe—"

"I know. If we have time in-between working at the café and planning your wedding."

"That wasn't exactly—"

"Don't worry." Zoe patted Lauren's hand. "With the three of us on the case, that killer has no hope of getting away with it."

"Brrt!"

CHAPTER 11

Lauren drove along the highway on Saturday afternoon. Zoe hummed a little tune, tapping her hands on her capri-clad knees.

"I guess we should do the wedding stuff first, then we can get ice cream from that amazing shop."

"Great idea." They were semi-regulars at a Sacramento store that created unusual flavors. Lauren's favorite so far was maple-rhubarb, while Zoe liked trying something different nearly every time.

Before they'd left, Lauren had set up Annie with a cyber play date with her pal AJ. Annie had discovered AJ as an abandoned kitten in the café's backyard. Ed had instantly fallen in love with the tiny brown tabby Maine Coon and adopted her. Now, AJ accompanied Ed when he volunteered at the animal shelter, and was friendly with some of the cats there.

By using the video function on her phone and calling Ed, who set up his own phone somewhere convenient for AJ to interact with, the two felines could see each on the screen and show their toys to each other. They also had "real" play dates as well.

"Maybe Mrs. Snuggle would like to have a cyber play date with Annie soon," Zoe mused, as Lauren chose the exit ramp.

"It would be good if it worked out. But Mrs. Snuggle didn't seem very interested in playing with Annie when we cat sat her."

"That's because she was moping for Father Mike," Zoe replied. "She might be ready to really make friends now. Father Mike was going to check if she was interested. I'll ask him about it."

"You could put it on your to-do list," Lauren teased.

"I will." Zoe pulled out her phone and started typing.

They parked and entered the department store.

Once they looked around for a few minutes, Lauren nodded. "I think this will be the best place if anyone wants to buy us a present."

"As soon as we fix up the details, we can add it to the invites, as well as the animal shelter info."

"Yes." They smiled at each other.

After approaching the gift registry clerk, Lauren gave her details.

"Do you have anything in mind you'd like to put on your wish list?" the thirty-something woman asked.

"Not really." She and Mitch hadn't spoken anymore about it.

"Ooh – what about this grill pan?" Zoe pointed to an impressive looking pan with ridges in the middle. "Mitch is pretty good at cooking steak."

"True." Lauren nodded. "Okay, that grill pan, please."

"What about a fancy spatula to go with it?" Zoe pointed again.

"Well, I guess."

"Wonderful." The clerk beamed at them. "Why don't you have a look around and come back with any other items you'd like to add to your list?"

By the time they'd had a quick browse, Zoe had convinced Lauren to add a large mixing bowl, a pizza cutter, and a pink and white plaid blanket. "It will go perfectly with the pink sofa," she enthused.

Lauren had to admit her cousin was right.

"You and Mitch can snuggle under it." Zoe winked. "And Annie can nest in it when she's not allowed in the bedroom." Her eyes lit up. "But you'll have a spare room when I move out. Maybe Annie could have it as her own room!"

Lauren's eyes widened. "I didn't even think of that. We can ask Annie and get her opinion."

They headed back to the counter and added to the wish list.

Zoe sighed. "I really do love that pink and white blanket."

"Why don't you buy one for yourself?" Lauren suggested. A thought struck her. "Am I supposed to give my maids of honor a present?"

"As one of them, I'll research that right now." Zoe pulled out her phone.

The sales clerk looked amused. Luckily, there were no other customers needing attention.

"Yes." Zoe showed her the article on the phone screen.

"Then I want to give you this blanket," Lauren replied.

"Really?" Zoe's face lit up. "But it's a bit expensive. I already checked the price tag."

"I don't care. Just promise me you'll use it."

"You know it." Zoe's eyes suddenly became a little shiny. "You're the best."

"No, you are."

"No, Annie is."

They both laughed.

Lauren paid for the blanket and the clerk gift-wrapped it for her.

"Make sure this blanket is at the top of the wish list, please," Zoe asked. "It would be awesome if we both had one."

"Will do." The clerk smiled.

They exited the store and walked a few blocks to the bridal shop, Zoe holding her tastefully wrapped blanket as if it cost a million dollars.

"What am I going to get Annie?" Lauren mused. "For her maid of honor gift?"

"We'll have to think of something wonderful," Zoe replied. "Ooh, look, there's the bridal shop!"

Luckily, it wasn't an overly warm day, and Lauren still felt reasonably fresh when they reached the store.

"Oh, no, it's closed." Zoe made a moue, gesturing to the handwritten sign on the door.

Closed for a personal emergency

"I hope nothing bad has happened," Lauren said.

"Yeah, like another murder." Zoe sobered. "Sorry, that wasn't funny."

Lauren patted her arm.

"At least we can look through the window." Zoe pressed her face against the glass. "I like these dresses."

Lauren admired an ivory satin gown with a sweetheart neckline.

"What are you doing here?"

Lauren turned at the sound of the female voice.

Brianna, the bride to be. She looked cool and summery in a white dress with tiny peach polka dots, and her blonde hair shimmered down her back.

"What are *you* doing here?" Zoe countered.

"I have a fitting in exactly one minute." Brianna tossed her head, her wavy locks bouncing.

"I think you're out of luck." Zoe pointed to the note on the door.

"No!" Brianna stamped her foot. "She *promised* me I could try on my gown again this afternoon. It was a teeny bit too big in the waist and she said she could alter it easily. What am I going to do now?"

"Maybe she left you a voice mail or text message?" Lauren suggested.

Brianna checked her fancy phone, covered in silver glitter. "Oh, she did send me a text. Her sister broke her ankle and she's taken her to the hospital. Couldn't her sister have called an ambulance instead?" Her eyes narrowed.

"Maybe they were together when it happened, and it was quicker to take her to the hospital herself," Lauren said. Her first impressions about Brianna seemed to have just been proven.

"So, are you still going to have your reception at Stately Vue Hall?" Zoe asked.

"Of course." Brianna nodded. "And now I have the Saturday I wanted."

"How did that happen?" Lauren asked curiously.

"Daddy fixed it."

"How did he do that?" Zoe probed.

"He made sure we were on Elizabeth's cancellation list and an opening suddenly popped up, right after Reginald was murdered." Brianna made it sound very innocent.

"Maybe the couple who originally had that date changed their mind after Reginald was killed," Lauren said slowly.

"Yeah." Zoe nodded.

"I don't care." Brianna shrugged. "I've got my dream date and that's all that matters. I'm going to have my dream dress, too." She pointed to the window. "You can't see my dress from here, but it's in there."

"How big is your wedding going to be?" Lauren asked curiously, wondering if Brianna would actually have three hundred guests.

"Big big."

For a moment, Lauren thought she sounded just like little Molly.

"Did the police question you about the murder?" Zoe asked.

"No. Daddy fixed it."

"How did he do that?" Lauren was curious to find out if her story tallied with Mitch's.

"He got our lawyer involved and the mean policeman went away." She shuddered. "He would definitely *not* get invited to my wedding." She eyed Lauren. "But your fiancé would."

"Thanks, but I think my fiancé would be too busy to attend," Lauren replied.

"Yeah, Mitch works a lot. So does my boyfriend Chris."

"I don't have to work," Brianna said. "But I go to school. It's so boring. Apart from being in the sorority. That's so much fun."

"What do your friends think about you getting married while you're still in college?" Lauren asked curiously.

"They think it's great! Daddy is going to buy me a house and Bobby will get the commission on it – he sells houses for Daddy – and Daddy's already promised to promote Bobby as long as he makes me happy."

"I hope he does make you happy," Lauren said, feeling a little sorry for Bobby. Did he know what he was getting into?

"Me too. He's already signed the pre-nup. And Daddy said I can have a cat just like yours." She eyed Lauren. "Can your cat have kittens?"

"No."

"Oh." Brianna sounded disappointed. "Never mind. I'll find one myself and Daddy will buy it for me."

Her phone rang, a high-pitched trill. "Bobby just sent a text, asking me how the dress fitting is going. I told him he had to read this book about how to be the perfect fiancé, and so far he's following the advice very well." She waved offhandedly to them and walked down the street, her gaze glued to her phone and her fingers busy.

"Poor Bobby," Zoe said.

"I think so."

"We might as well get ice cream now," Zoe declared.

"I guess." She was looking forward to the frozen treat, but was disappointed that the dress shop was closed.

"We could come back here next weekend," Zoe suggested.

"I'd like that." Lauren smiled. "We could call first to make sure the proprietor is here. I hope her sister will be okay."

"Yeah." Zoe nodded.

They walked to the ice-cream shop, which wasn't far.

"I can't decide." Zoe's gaze roved over all the unusual flavors. "I've had coconut and matcha, plum and espresso – ooh, mocha raspberry! I don't remember that flavor."

"It's new," the teenager behind the counter informed her.

"I'll have one scoop of that, and one of—" Zoe tapped her cheek "—pineapple dragon fruit!"

"I don't think I've heard of dragon fruit." Lauren's gaze skimmed that particular flavor, which was a pale yellow.

"It tastes like a pear combined with a kiwifruit," the teen told them.

"I think I'll stick with one scoop of maple-rhubarb please." Lauren made her selection, mindful of her upcoming wedding dress shopping.

"Mmm." Zoe dug into her ice-cream. "I really love this mocha raspberry, but I'm thinking this pineapple dragon fruit is a tiny bit acidic."

"That's interesting." Lauren peered at her cousin's choice. "I love this maple rhubarb."

"I know you do." Zoe grinned. "Hey, don't you think it was weird we bumped into Brianna just now?"

"Yes." Lauren nodded, then enjoyed another mouthful of her treat. "But I guess it makes sense. She'll need a gown if she's getting married next month, and although I haven't checked the online reviews for the bridal shop, it must be very popular."

"Yeah, especially if Brooke recommended it and Brianna knows about it as well. But do you think it's weird she's suddenly gotten the exact date she wanted?"

"Yes, I do think it's a bit strange." Lauren thought back. "Do you remember what her dad said when we were there at Stately Vue Hall the first time? He said to Reginald something like, "*Is there any way we can fix this? Name your price.*"

"Hey, yeah." Zoe clicked her fingers. "You're right."

They stared at each other. Only a trickle of cold melting ice-cream on her fingers alerted Lauren to the fact she hadn't finished her treat.

"Brianna killed Reginald!" Zoe declared.

"You think?" Lauren finished off the maple-rhubarb before it got messier.

"Who else? You saw how she was when Reginald didn't instantly give her the date she wanted. So BAM! She killed him."

"How?"

"We know how. She hit him over the head and stuffed him into the hedge."

"She doesn't look that strong," Lauren said doubtfully.

"I'm sure she does Pilates and core exercises and all that." Zoe waved a hand in the air. "She mightn't look it, but I bet she's super strong on the inside. Plus, being mad because she couldn't get what she wanted for the first time in her life would have given her the extra oomph to get the job done."

"You mean the murder."

"Yeah." Zoe sobered.

"What was Reginald doing in the knot garden at that time of day, anyway?" Lauren asked. "He must have known we had an appointment with him."

"Didn't I say a while ago that maybe he had a hush-hush super-secret appointment with someone that no one else knew about and it turned sour?"

Lauren thought back. "Yes, you did. Sorry, with all the wedding planning—"

"I know." Zoe patted her arm. "It's okay. This investigation hasn't received my full attention either." She looked glum for a second. "I don't know why it had to happen now – during one of the most exciting times of our – your life."

"Yeah." Now Lauren sounded glum.

"So it's either Brianna or the super-secret person who did it."

"What about Elizabeth?"

"You have a point." Zoe nodded. "Okay, three people could have done it."

"What if," Lauren said slowly, "Elizabeth killed Reginald because of her cancellation list? We don't know how much Brianna's dad was willing to pay to get that dream date in August."

Zoe's eyes widened. "It could be enough to kill for! We know he's loaded."

"Or seems to be." Lauren knew that sometimes appearances were deceptive.

"And Reginald sounded shocked when Brianna's dad tried to bribe him."

"True."

"And it must be annoying having to work with your ex-husband every day and be reminded that your marriage didn't work out," Zoe added.

"Mmm." Lauren didn't know if she would be able to do it if that happened to her and Mitch. *Not that it would.*

"I wouldn't like to do that." Zoe sounded certain.

Lauren nodded.

"So, Elizabeth is fed up with having to put up with Reginald, is tempted by George's – that is Brianna's dad's name, right? – offer—"

"Bribe," Lauren put in.

“Bribe, and kills him. Then she either persuades the other couple who’ve already nabbed the dream Saturday in August to cancel, telling them it would be bad karma or something—”

“—or bribes them herself with a small percentage of what George offered her,” Lauren added thoughtfully.

“Yeah!” Zoe looked like she wanted to jump up from the bench and pace. “Or she could offer them an upgraded wedding package for no extra cost if they take that Tuesday in October or postpone their wedding to another Saturday—”

“Which is next February.”

“I bet they have a huge markup on these menu prices, so it’s not like Elizabeth would lose much money by offering an upgrade,” Zoe said. “Not like the bistro where we’re having our – your reception. You’re getting a really good deal.”

“I know.” Lauren smiled.

“But to bring us back to the killer, that could be why Elizabeth killed

Reginald. Even if she bribed the other couple who had Brianna's dream Saturday, there'd still be plenty of money left for her from George's offer. I'm guessing."

"I think this is a really good theory." Lauren glanced at her cousin.

"We should definitely tell Mitch."

"You mean Detective Castern."

"Yuck."

"I know." Lauren sighed. "I don't think he'll be receptive to us suggesting this to him, even if he is looking at Elizabeth and Myrna."

"What about Myrna?" Zoe tapped her cheek. "We haven't really talked much about her."

"That's true. But you're not trying to avoid Detective Castern, are you?"

"Maybe," Zoe admitted. "Why don't you tell Mitch our theory and he can tell us if we're close to what Castern is thinking?"

"If he knows what that man is thinking," Lauren replied. She pulled her phone out of her purse and speed-dialed her fiancé. Every time she thought of Mitch that way, she still got a thrill in her heart, even though they'd been engaged for six months now.

Mitch answered, and she quickly told them their thoughts about Elizabeth being the killer.

He promised to talk about it that evening with her, proposing dinner at the cottage – with Zoe and Chris.

"Chris is free?" Lauren asked.

"His shift got cancelled at the last minute. I don't think Zoe knows yet."

"I can't wait to tell her." Lauren smiled. She ended the call and turned to her cousin. "Want to have a double dinner tonight?"

CHAPTER 12

"Pizza. Or chili, but that might take too long. Or burgers from Gary's. Or steak that Mitch can cook. Or—"

"How about we ask the guys for their opinion as well?" Lauren teased. They walked back to the car.

Zoe's phone buzzed. "Chris says I can choose." She grinned. "It's awesome his shift got cancelled. He's worked a lot lately." Her tone sobered. "It will be good for him to have a break."

Lauren nodded. She knew her cousin had serious feelings for Chris, and was pretty sure they were returned.

"Pizza?" She looked at Zoe.

"You know it."

They got in the car and Lauren started the ignition.

"So next Saturday afternoon we'll come back here for ice-cream – and wedding dress shopping," Zoe declared.

"What about your maid of honor outfit?" A sudden thought struck Lauren. "You'll need a dress as well. Am I the worst bride in the world for just realizing?" Her cheeks grew hot.

"No, you're not." Zoe scrunched her nose. "I was going to talk to you about that. I'm happy to wear a dress if you want me to, but I haven't worn one for a long time."

Lauren stared at her, images of Zoe's outfits flickering before her eyes.

"That's true. I hadn't realized. You can wear anything you want."

"Really?"

"Of course."

"Thanks." Zoe grinned. "I'll take a look when we go shopping for your gown and see what they have. Maybe I *will* like wearing a dress for your wedding."

They drove home. Annie greeted them, her cyber play date with AJ over.

"Mitch and Chris are coming over tonight," Lauren told her.

"Brrt!" Annie waved her plumy silver tail in the air.

"I can't wait to show Chris my co-maid of honor gift." Zoe stroked the shiny gift wrapping. "I didn't get any ice cream drips on it, either."

"Brrt!" *That's good.*

"You can open it now if you like," Lauren suggested. "I don't know if that's the traditional way or not, but—"

"Sometimes we're not traditional." Zoe beamed. Her fingers paused when she started to tackle the decorative bow. "Maybe I should wait until Chris is here so he can duly admire it."

"Good idea." Lauren turned to Annie. "I'm going to give you a present as well, for being my maid of honor along with Zoe. Is there anything you would really like?"

"Brrt," Annie said thoughtfully.

"Maybe she needs to think about it for a bit," Zoe commented.

"I understand. Just let me know when you've decided what you'd like, Annie."

"Brrt." *I will.*

Lauren grabbed a shower, then Zoe. After being out in the warm July air for a few hours, she definitely felt hot and sticky.

Finally deciding on casual linen pants and a flattering lightweight apricot top, she was ready for pizza night.

She quickly brushed her hair and joined Annie and Zoe in the living room. Zoe had changed into another pair of capris and a black and white t-shirt.

"I hope the guys hurry up. I think I'm getting a bit hangry." Zoe grabbed her phone. "Do you think we should order the pizza now or wait until they get here?"

The doorbell chimed.

"I think you've got your answer."

Mitch and Chris stood on the porch. Although Mitch sometimes stayed overnight, he didn't have his own key, despite their engagement. Lauren wondered if they should talk about that.

"Hi." Mitch kissed her tenderly as he came in.

"Hi." She smiled up at him, then turned her attention to his friend. "Hi, Chris."

"Hi." He smiled, before he was nearly bowled over by Zoe. His even, attractive features lit up at the spontaneous embrace.

"I've missed you." She reached up to kiss him.

When he was able to, Chris bent down to the feline. "Hi, Annie."

"Brrt." *Hi, Chris.*

"I've brought Annie a special dinner." Mitch held out a little cooler bag. "Some sirloin I cut up at home. I know she likes it."

"Brrt!" *Thank you!* Annie led the way to the kitchen, looking up at Mitch expectantly.

"Annie would like her dinner now." Zoe giggled.

"I think so."

"Does Annie want you to give it to her or would she like me to?" Mitch asked.

"I think she's happy for you to put it in her bowl," Lauren replied. When she'd first met Mitch, he'd told her he'd had little to do with cats his whole life, and it had taken him a while to get used to interacting with Annie. Now, her heart warmed at his thoughtfulness toward her fur baby.

Annie's pink tongue darted out, as if savoring the first taste of raw meat, then she ate enthusiastically.

"Brrt!" She licked the bowl clean.

"Now it's our turn for dinner." Zoe waved her phone in the air.

They ordered their favorite pizzas from the local pizza shop. A Lauren special, comprised of Canadian bacon, mushroom, and sundried tomato, and several Zoe specials, a combination of sausage and pepperoni, as the guys enjoyed that one as well.

"Look what Lauren gave me. It's my co-maid of honor gift." Zoe turned to Chris, showing him the prettily wrapped parcel.

There was a slight look of panic in Mitch's eye. "Do I need to give *you* a gift?" he asked Chris.

Chris checked his phone. "This article says yes." He showed the screen to Mitch.

"What sort of thing?" Zoe asked.

"Cufflinks or something like that," Chris answered.

The paper crackled as Zoe unwrapped the present carefully.

"Isn't it beautiful?" Zoe stroked the pink and white plaid blanket.

"It is," Chris agreed, wrapping his arm around her shoulder.

"That would look good with your sofa," Mitch commented, gesturing toward the living room.

"It's at the top of our registry list," Lauren said. "I hope it won't be too much pink for you."

"Not yet." He chuckled.

"As soon as I saw it, I wanted one for myself." Zoe continued to stroke the soft woolen fabric.

"Brrt!" Annie jumped up on one of the kitchen chairs and peered at the blanket. She reached out a paw and patted it carefully.

"I think Annie approves." Zoe giggled.

The pizzas arrived, and they ate in the kitchen, Annie keeping them company. The scent and taste of the bacon and pepperoni, as well as the fragrant tomato sauce, honed their appetites.

Lauren and Zoe told Mitch about bumping into Brianna that afternoon.

"I can totally see her as a killer." Zoe finished a slice of pizza. "I think she might be capable of anything if it stood in the way of her dream wedding."

"I think Zoe could be right," Lauren agreed, pushing her plate away. The pizza had been delicious but she was feeling full right now.

Zoe reached for another piece, this time a Lauren special. She winked at her cousin.

"Castern is still looking at Elizabeth and Myrna," Mitch said.

"Has he gotten anywhere?" Chris asked.

"Not as far as I know." Mitch shook his head.

"What about Myrna?" Lauren asked.

"Yeah, we haven't really thought about her much," Zoe admitted. "But maybe she killed Reginald."

"Why?" Mitch asked.

"Because … because … George, Brianna's dad, bribed her! Yeah, he bribed her to free up that Saturday in August and the only way she thought that would happen would be if she killed her boss!"

"But she'd still have to work with Elizabeth to make that Saturday work for Brianna's wedding," Mitch pointed out.

"She split the money with Elizabeth! He bribed Myrna instead of Elizabeth."

"And Elizabeth didn't mind that Myrna killed her ex-husband?" Mitch asked.

"Probably not," Zoe replied.

"I'm guessing if Myrna did do it, she didn't tell Elizabeth," Chris spoke. "Maybe she said afterward, by the way, Brianna's dad has offered me a lot of money if we can make that dream August Saturday happen, and since you're my boss, it's only fair if I share it with you."

"That could happen," Lauren said slowly.

"I knew we made a good team." Zoe smiled at Chris.

"It's a theory I would look at," Mitch admitted, "but unfortunately I'm not in charge of the case."

"How is *your* case going?" Lauren asked.

"I think I've finally got a lead. I'll look into it more on Monday."

"Who knew there were croquet thieves in Gold Leaf Valley?" Zoe shook her head.

"As long as there aren't any cupcake thieves," Chris joked. "I don't know what I'd do without yours, Lauren."

They all laughed, Annie adding a little chirp that sounded like a cat giggle.

"I guess we should talk about the wedding," Zoe announced. "Now you two have the date and venue organized, we can send out the invitations."

"We can do them on the computer," Lauren said. "Now I've finally decided on a pink and violet floral design." She turned to Mitch. "You did say I could choose."

He nodded.

"I've done a mockup of one on my phone." Lauren showed the screen to Mitch. "What do you think?"

"It looks good." He smiled, his brown eyes crinkling at the corners. He handed the phone to Chris.

"That's really thoughtful, asking for donations to the local animal shelter in lieu of a present," he said, handing the device across the table to Zoe.

"I'd love to make all the gifts a donation to the shelter, but some guests might be disappointed if they couldn't give us an actual present," Lauren said.

"We thought this would be the best option." Zoe handed the phone back to Lauren.

"This is our wedding invitation." Lauren showed her fur baby the pretty design.

"Brrt." Annie stared at the display.

"Don't forget to think about what you'd like for your co-maid of honor gift," Zoe said. "We can show you some photos of toys, or baskets, or blankets, or—"

"Brrt." Annie gently touched her paw to the screen.

"Oh, that's a good idea." Lauren saw where the feline's paw touched the wording in the invitation. "We could buy you a toy or whatever you'd like from the animal shelter, so they get part of the proceeds." She knew they sold gift items for pets there.

"Brrp." *No.* She tapped her paw on the screen again.

"*Donations to the local animal shelter in lieu of a gift would be wonderful*", Lauren read out.

"Brrt!" Annie seemed to nod her head.

"You mean you'd like your gift to be a donation to the animal shelter, Annie?" Chris asked.

"Brrt!" *Yes!*

"Oh, Annie." Lauren's heart swelled with love for her fur baby. "That is such a kind thing to do."

"Definitely." Zoe nodded. "You're so thoughtful, Annie."

The guys agreed, smiles on their faces.

"Then that's what we'll do," Lauren declared. "Your co-maid of honor gift will be a donation to the animal shelter, where Ed volunteers."

"Brrt!"

CHAPTER 13

The next day, the four of them attended church, Father Mike beaming at seeing them in the congregation.

Afterward, Zoe had lunch with Chris, before going to the pottery studio, while Lauren and Mitch went to the local vineyard, one of their favorite places.

As they enjoyed lunch in the outdoor café, Lauren told him about Zoe's proposal.

"Do you mind if Zoe moves into your apartment after we're married?"

"No." Mitch sounded as if he loved the idea.

"She thought she could take over your lease once you move in with me."

"That shouldn't be a problem." He nodded. "And the rent isn't too bad – she could probably swing it."

"I hope so." Lauren crinkled her brow. "I hadn't thought of that. Maybe

I should give her a raise – Ed as well."

"Can you afford to?"

"Probably." Lauren thought about the state of the café's books. "Things are going well at the moment and I have a decent balance in the business account."

"It would be good if it's just the three of us in the cottage – you, me, and Annie."

"I know." She let herself savor that image for a second. "But Zoe will be over for dinner maybe a few times per week, and we still have craft club Friday nights." She thought she should warn him.

"I know Zoe is important to you, and so is craft club." His fingers were warm against her own as they held hands across the table. "And I want you to be happy."

"And I want you to be happy." She smiled at him.

"I am," he assured her.

***

That afternoon, Lauren printed out the wedding invitations. The paper had arrived earlier that week, so all she had to do was print a sample first, to make sure the words were centered properly.

Mitch had gone home, saying he would start packing up some of his stuff, even though there were several weeks until their ceremony.

The test invitation looked perfect.

"Brrt?" Annie stood on her back legs when she heard the whirr of the printer, and stretched up as the paper came out.

"It's the first wedding invitation." She showed her the paper decorated with pink and violet flowers.

"Brrt," Annie said in approval.

"Now we have to print out the rest of them."

Annie 'supervised' the printing of the remaining fifty-three invitations.

There were sixteen sheets of paper left, just in case they had any last-minute additions to the guest list.

"Now we have to put them in envelopes and address them."

Lauren wished Zoe was here to help her for this bit. She thought it would be just as quick to write the addresses by hand than to type each name into the word processing program and then center each envelope perfectly – and she wasn't sure if printing guests' names and addresses would be frowned upon as a faux pas, anyway.

By the time Zoe arrived home that evening, Lauren had finished over half the envelopes.

"Ooh, your handwriting is so nice and even." Zoe admired the pale pink envelopes.

"Thanks." Lauren stretched out her fingers, which were feeling cramped. "I think I'll have to finish the rest tomorrow."

"Just as well we're not going dress shopping until next weekend."

"How was the pottery studio?" Lauren asked.

"Great." Zoe grinned. "Chris came with me and let me boss him around as my assistant." She giggled. "But don't worry, I'll make sure the mugs will be ready for the wedding."

"I wasn't worried." Lauren smiled. "I spoke to Mitch and it's okay with him if you'd like to move into his apartment after the wedding. But if you've changed your mind, you're welcome to keep living here." She was sure Mitch would understand if her cousin didn't want to move.

"I haven't." Zoe shook her head.

"I should have done this before, but I want to give you and Ed a small raise."

"Really?" Zoe's face lit up.

"Really," Lauren confirmed. "The accounts are going pretty well at the moment, so I should be able to swing it."

"Awesome!"

"You might have to thank Martha." Lauren smiled.

"Yeah, her marshmallow lattes are a hit, and we're making an extra profit with the marshmallow fee." Zoe giggled.

"A little profit." Lauren thought of the thirty cents that covered the cost of those pink and white marshmallows and a little for the café.

"And your carrot cupcakes."

"I'm going to make a batch every day this coming week."

"Good idea."

"Brrt!"

***

The next day, Lauren and Zoe went grocery shopping, visited Mrs. Finch, and then Zoe zoomed off to the pottery studio, borrowing Lauren's car, while Lauren mixed up cupcake batter for Tuesday, and labored over the rest of the wedding invitation envelopes, Annie 'supervising.'

"Finished." Lauren relaxed in the chair and gazed at her handiwork. She hoped this would be her only marriage because right now she didn't want to handwrite another address *ever.*

She wriggled her right hand, her fingers feeling cramped.

"Brrt?" Annie gently patted one of the envelopes.

"Now all we have to do is fold the invitations and put them in the envelopes." Thank goodness the envelopes were self-sealing.

She wondered what Mitch was doing right now, knowing it would have nothing to do with wedding stationery. She envied him for a minute, then reminded herself how lucky she was to have found him. Or had Annie found him for her? She glanced at her fur baby, picked her up, and cuddled her close.

"Thank you for being you," she murmured.

"Brrt." Annie snuggled into her chest.

Lauren nearly dozed off, jerking awake when she heard the back door slam.

"I'm back," Zoe called out. "Now I've made good progress on the pottery mugs, we can start sleuthing!"

CHAPTER 14

"Sleuthing?" Lauren blinked, and placed Annie down on the floor. "We've got the café tomorrow."

"After the café." Zoe flapped a hand. She spied the invitations. "Have you finished them?"

"Yes."

"Awesome. That means we can definitely go sleuthing tomorrow!"

"But—"

"It will still be light when we close at five," Zoe continued, "and if we don't have any customers after four-thirty, we could close a teensy bit early, and–"

"Who are we investigating?"

"Oh, you know, Myrna, Elizabeth, Brianna, George, and Bobby."

"Bobby?"

"Why not? Maybe he's so terrified of Brianna being mad about not getting her dream Saturday wedding date next month that he killed

Reginald because he was standing in her way."

"Do you really think that's a theory?" Lauren stared at her cousin.

"We'll know after we talk to him."

"Brrt!"

***

The next morning, Lauren stuck stamps on the envelopes as she crunched granola, careful not to get any crumbs or milk on them.

"I can post these before we open the café."

"Do you think that many invites will fit in our mail box?" Zoe frowned.

"No. So I'll hurry over to the post office straight after breakfast."

"Brrt." Annie sounded approving. She sat on the kitchen chair next to Lauren's, watching with wide green eyes.

"This might be the perfect time to tell Annie about—" Zoe dropped her voice and stage-whispered "—getting her own room."

"Brrt?" Annie looked enquiringly at both of them.

"When Mitch and I get married," Lauren started to explain, "Zoe will be moving out."

"Brrt?" *Why?*

"So I don't cramp their style." Zoe winked at the silver-gray tabby. "But I'll be over here all the time, and all three of us will still work at the café."

"That's right." Lauren hoped she sounded reassuring. "So, we were thinking, would you like to have Zoe's bedroom as your own?"

"Brrp." Annie sounded like she was thinking about it.

"You can still share my bedroom with Mitch. At times," she added hastily.

"Yeah, not when they're kissing and all that stuff." Zoe giggled.

Annie looked like she was thinking things over.

"Or else you could keep hanging out on the sofa at night," Lauren suggested. "You have that lovely pink velvet cushion Mitch gave you."

"And if someone gives Lauren a pink and white blanket just like mine, you might be able to use that as well," Zoe said.

"Brrp." Annie jumped off the chair and trotted out of the room.

Lauren and Zoe looked at each other.

"Let's follow her." Zoe zipped after the feline.

Annie headed into Zoe's bedroom, looking around.

"You'll have a people bed to curl up on." Zoe indicated the twin bed. "I thought I could buy a futon when I move into Mitch's apartment."

"Good idea." She knew Mitch had complained about needing a new bed at times, and since hers was in good shape, he'd decided to take his to the dump when he moved out.

Annie leaped onto the bed with the purple bedspread, turned around in a ball, and settled down.

"I think she's testing it for comfort." Zoe giggled. A thought seemed to hit her. "What are you going to do if you and Mitch—" She held her hands above her belly in an up and down motion.

"Have a baby?" Lauren whispered. She and Mitch had decided they wanted children but hadn't spoken about a timeline yet. "I don't know."

"I bet Annie would love having a sister – or a brother – a human one." Zoe beamed.

"Probably," Lauren allowed.

"But if that happens, and Annie wants this to be her bedroom, then where will I put the baby?"

"The junk room?" Zoe raised an eyebrow.

"Yes." Lauren let out the breath she didn't know she'd been holding.

"I think Mitch is going to be very busy after he moves in, cleaning out that room. I guess that's what husbands are for!" Zoe erupted into a fit of giggles.

"Among other things." Lauren joined in the laughter.

Annie opened her eyes, as if wondering what was going on.

"I've got to get these envelopes finished." Lauren checked her watch. She'd have to hurry.

"I'll meet you and Annie at the café." She placed all the invitations into a tote bag, blew Annie a kiss, and raced out of the house.

She rushed down the street to the post office, mailed all the envelopes, and rushed back to the café. Barely after eight-thirty. Good.

Zoe and Annie were already in there, her cousin unstacking chairs and Annie strolling around the room, as if on the lookout for anything that had been left out of place from Saturday, even though they'd cleaned before locking up that day.

Lauren waved to them, then headed into the kitchen.

"Hi, Ed."

"Hi." He looked up from the pastry he was shaping. "What's up?"

"I'd like to give you a raise."

"That would be great." He smiled. "Thanks."

"It's only a small one." She felt she should point that out.

"No worries. I know you pay as much as you can."

"Thanks." She returned his smile. "I posted the invitations this morning, so you should get yours in a day or so."

"I'll look forward to it."

She quickly put some cupcakes into the oven, then returned to the café. Zoe had unstacked all the chairs and was checking the register.

"I don't think I needed to rush so much after all," she admitted, sinking onto the stool behind the counter for a second.

"Annie and I have it all under control." Zoe grinned. "Don't worry."

"Thanks." She glanced over at the pink cat bed where Annie sat up straight, all her senses seemingly on alert.

Switching on the espresso machine, she decided to make herself a quick latte.

"Want something?" she asked her cousin.

"A marshmallow one would be great." Zoe's eyes lit up. "Has Ed tried one?"

"I don't think so."

Soon the aroma of hazelnut and spices filled the air when she ground the beans for each cup.

"I love this latte." Zoe spooned up some pink and white froth, a blissful smile on her face.

Lauren took Ed's surprise beverage into the kitchen. "Tell me what you think." She placed it on the workbench.

He eyed it suspiciously. "Is this Martha's latte?"

"Yes."

He took a tentative sip. "Not bad." He nodded. "Thanks."

Lauren checked her carrot cupcakes, taking them out from the oven. "I'll frost them when they've cooled down."

He nodded.

The morning disappeared in a rush of customers.

Mrs. Finch came in, and so did Ms. Tobin, Hans, Martha, and Claire and little Molly.

Each time, Lauren and Zoe told them they should receive their wedding invitations in a couple of days. Everyone seemed delighted.

"I can't wait until we close this afternoon," Zoe told her after lunch. They'd each grabbed a quick lunch in the cottage, but now there was a short lull.

"Are you sure it's a good idea?" Lauren eyed her cousin doubtfully.

"Yes," Zoe insisted. "I've thought up the perfect cover story for us. You and Mitch are thinking of buying another property, and you see something you like and BANG! in we go to George's real estate office to inquire about that particular property."

She showed Lauren the website on her phone.

"We can't afford any of these." Lauren shook her head in dismay. She knew she was lucky to have inherited her Gramms' cottage and café, but now, looking at the prices on the site – some over a million dollars – she realized just how fortunate she was.

"He doesn't know that. Neither does Bobby." Zoe flapped a hand.

“But he might have overheard Reginald calling me a budget bride.” Lauren was still getting over that term.

“But Bobby wasn’t there,” Zoe argued. “So, I thought we could see if Bobby *is* there, and pretend we’re interested in finding somewhere for you and Mitch to live.”

“But why would we want to live in Sacramento when the café is here?”

“Semantics,” Zoe said airily. “Leave it all to me.”

“That’s what I’m afraid of.”

“It will be fine. You’ll see.”

***

They closed the café just before five. To Zoe’s dismay, a couple of customers came in at four-thirty for a late afternoon caffeine fix, and bought some of the last few cupcakes. She let out a sigh of relief when they didn’t tarry.

“Oh, good, carrot cake for dinner.” Zoe bagged up the two remaining treats when they closed. Everything else had sold out.

Lauren wondered if people were tiring of her new creation already, then reminded herself she'd made a double batch that morning.

"We could have salad for our first course," she teased, trooping down the private hallway with Zoe and Annie. They'd decided to leave Annie at home, instead of exposing her to the warm summer temperature outside.

"I guess," Zoe reluctantly agreed. "Or, we could stop for burgers and fries on the way home." She looked like she definitely preferred that idea.

"I have bridal gown shopping next weekend," she reminded her.

"So?" Zoe looked at her quizzically. "You look exactly the same to me. In fact, all this rushing around we've been doing has probably burned up extra calories and you might have lost a little weight."

Lauren didn't know if that theory was actually true, but she decided she liked the sound of it.

"Okay." She gave in. "That does seem like a good idea."
Lauren fed Annie, spent a few minutes with her, then said goodbye. "We'll be back later this evening."
"We shouldn't be too late," Zoe added. "And then we can watch TV together."
"You can choose," Lauren promised her fur baby.
"Brrt!"

***

"Is the real estate office going to be open by the time we get there?" Lauren asked, choosing an exit ramp.
"I already checked. They're open late. They probably don't want to miss out on any prospective buyers."
"I wonder how many hours Bobby works each day?"
"Probably lots," Zoe replied, "to make a good impression on the boss, who will also be his father-in-law." She sounded a little sorry for Bobby.
"What if Bobby isn't working today?"

"Hmm. I hadn't thought of that. Well, if he isn't, we can talk to George instead. He's on my list, anyway."

"He is?"

"Everyone connected to that day is on my list," Zoe admitted.

With Zoe reading out directions from her phone, they found their way to the real estate office without too much trouble.

"Park there!" Zoe pointed to a space a few doors down.

"That was lucky." Lauren turned off the ignition.

"Ooh – look!" Zoe opened her car door and raced off.

"Zoe!" Lauren locked the car and hurried after her cousin, her eyes widening as she saw Myrna coming out of the real estate office. No wonder Zoe had exited the car in such a rush.

"Hi, Myrna," she heard her cousin greet the assistant from Stately Vue Hall. "Whatever are you doing here?"

Lauren admired Zoe's acting skills. Maybe that was why she'd been cast as head elf in one of the town's Christmas plays.

The assistant blushed, pink spots of color in her pale cheeks. She wore office attire of a gray skirt and white blouse, the same kind of outfit she wore the previous week.

"I've been looking for a condo to buy. I've recently come into an inheritance."

"Really?" Zoe asked. "Aren't they expensive, like over three-hundred thousand dollars? Even more than that for new construction?"

Her cousin had done her homework.

"George said he could get me a good deal." She gestured to the real estate window. "He said he works directly with some of the developers."

"You must have a big inheritance," Zoe said.

"I've also saved up for years," Myrna replied.

"Did you see anything you liked?" Lauren asked.

"Yes, there's one place that's gorgeous, but it's just a little too expensive, even with a big down payment and a small mortgage." She hesitated. "I don't want to overextend myself."

"I understand," Lauren replied. And she did.

"Maybe George can put some feelers out and find you something just as good but for a lower price," Zoe suggested.

"Maybe," Myrna replied.

"What about Bobby? Is he in there right now?"

"Yes, he was at his desk a few minutes ago." Myrna sounded puzzled.

"I thought we could ask him to show us some possibilities," Zoe said. "Lauren and Mitch are looking for a new property."

"Well – good luck." Myrna's phone chimed with a beat of classical music. She stared at the screen. "I'm sorry, I have to go."

"Of course." Lauren nodded to her.

"Come on." Zoe practically pulled her through the glass door.

The office was light and airy, with big wooden desks, and photos featuring impressive homes with beautiful landscaping. A welcome blast of icy air stirred her shoulder-length hair.

"Can I help you?" Bobby. His hair looked a little short, as if he'd just had it cut. He seemed to be the only person in the office.

Lauren recognized him from Brianna's photo.

"You must be Bobby." Zoe thrust out her hand. "Brianna's told us so much about you."

"She has?" He looked surprised and pleased.

"She said you're the best real estate guy here," Zoe enthused. "My cousin Lauren is getting married – we met Brianna and her dad at Stately Vue Hall – and she recommended we see you if we're in the market for a new home. Well, Lauren and her fiancé Mitch are."

Lauren stared at Zoe. This seemed more than a basic cover story.

"In fact, Lauren likes this house." Zoe showed him her phone. "And it says you're the listing agent." She beamed at him.

"Of course." Bobby ushered them over to his large desk. "Anything for a friend of Brianna's. I can definitely show you this home. Let's see." He pulled up information on his computer. "How about tomorrow at eleven a.m.?"

"Actually, I think this property might be too big for us," Lauren apologized. "It says it has five bedrooms and four bathrooms." She looked at the listing sheet Bobby had placed in front of her, wondering why their cover story involved *her* house hunting and not Zoe.

"I have some smaller houses that are just as nice." Bobby clacked away on the keyboard. "There's a sweet three bedroom with two and half baths just around the block from the other house and it has a nice garden."

"Let's see." Zoe hurried around so she stood behind Bobby. "Ooh, yeah, that does look cute. Lauren, come look."

She reluctantly rose and joined them behind Bobby's desk, feeling guilty at their subterfuge. "Ohh."

All feelings of guilt disappeared for a second. An older style brick home with a beautiful but small garden met her gaze. She could just picture herself and Mitch walking hand-in-hand in the garden. Then she glanced at the price and paled.

"I knew you'd like it." Zoe winked at her behind Bobby's back.

Lauren resumed her seat facing Bobby. "I'm sorry, that house is gorgeous, but I'm afraid I can't afford it."

"Not even with your fiancé?" Bobby sounded disappointed.

"Not even," Lauren replied a little glumly. "I think we're wasting your time. We should go."

"No!" Zoe protested. "I'm sure Bobby can find us something. What about a cute condo, like Myrna was looking at just now?"

"You know Myrna?" Bobby looked surprised. "Oh yeah, you would if you're getting married at the same place Brianna and I am."

"We're not getting married there." Lauren didn't want to be totally dishonest with him. He seemed like a nice guy.

"We did go and check it out," Zoe added. "But with the murder and everything—"

"That was terrible." Bobby shook his head. "I asked Brianna if she wanted to cancel the reception there and go somewhere else, but she said that venue was her dream place and so was the date of Saturday, August fourteenth, and we *had* to get married there."

"She showed us her awesome engagement ring," Zoe continued. "Did you buy it for her?"

"Of course." Bobby nodded. "Brianna picked it out herself. I'd saved for years, even in high school, so I could help my parents pay for my college tuition and so I'd get a head start buying my own home one day, but the proudest day of my life was when I slid that diamond ring on Brianna's finger – even though I spent all my savings on it."

"How did you two meet?" Zoe asked.

"Brianna came into the office, looking for her dad. He wasn't here, so I kept her company until he returned. Then she asked me out to dinner." He looked bashful.

"I hope she appreciates you," Lauren said. Was he so infatuated with Brianna that he couldn't see she was a spoiled brat? Or did she act differently around him and he saw the real her?

"I think so." He flushed. "Otherwise, why would she marry me? I couldn't believe it when she said yes, but she did. And now she's organizing the wedding."

"She's not hiring a wedding planner?" Zoe probed.

"Yeah, she did, at first, but she fired them. Said they didn't have a clue and she could do a better job. She's got a scrap book that she started when she was twelve, with pages torn out of magazines, to help her."

"What sort of pages?" Zoe asked.

"Wedding dresses, shoes, china patterns, that sort of thing," Bobby replied.

"So, Myrna's condo," Zoe prompted after a moment, resuming her seat facing Bobby.

"It's in this recent development." Bobby handed them a paper listing.

"I can see why she likes it." Zoe nodded.

"Unfortunately, I'm not sure if she'll go ahead with the purchase." Bobby sounded disappointed for Myrna. "The condo fees are on the high side."

"Even with a big inheritance?" Zoe looked at Bobby inquisitively.

"I don't know anything about that." His tone was a little prim.

"It's a shame if she can't afford it." Lauren could see why Myrna had taken a liking to the building, with its wooden shutters and slight Swiss chalet village vibe.

"Myrna said George promised her a good deal on a condo." Zoe looked around the empty office. "Is he here?"

"No. He had to go out," Bobby answered.

"That's too bad."

"Let me know if there are any other properties you'd like to see." He handed them a card.

"Thank you." Lauren felt guilty at wasting his time.

"Good luck with the wedding," Zoe told him.

"I'm the luckiest man in the world." His face lit up. "Sometimes I wonder why Brianna chose me, when she could have her pick of guys, but she says I'm her Bobby Bob." He blushed when he uttered the pet name.

They said goodbye to him and walked back to the car.

"Poor Bobby." Zoe fastened her seatbelt. "He seems like a good guy."

"Maybe Brianna is different when she's with him?" Lauren offered.

"I hope so, like one-hundred-and-eighty degrees different," Zoe joked. Then she sobered. "It looks like

Myrna gave Bobby the same cover story – she's come into money and wants to buy a condo."

"Perhaps it's true." Lauren drove along the highway. "She could have been mentioned in a will."

"Or Brianna's dad George bribed her with enough money that she could afford to buy a condo – maybe."

They stopped for burgers and fries at a fast-food place halfway home.

"Mmm." Zoe munched on her beef. "Not as good as Gary's in Gold Leaf Valley, though."

"No."

"We can eat the cupcakes when we get home."

"Good idea." Lauren only ate half her bun and had ordered the smallest serving of fries, and a diet soda. Feeling a little virtuous, she told herself that one cupcake couldn't hurt – she hoped.

When they arrived home, they enjoyed their carrot cakes, explaining to Annie about their sleuthing, then let her choose their evening's entertainment. It was the movie about the princess who discovers her whole life is a lie apart from being a princess. Lauren stifled a groan as she settled down to watch it for possibly the tenth time in six months.

CHAPTER 15

The next morning, Mitch stopped by the café as soon as they opened.

"Hi." He leaned across the counter and kissed her.

"Hi."

"I'm sorry I didn't call you last night, but I finally cracked the croquet case."

"You did?" Zoe joined them.

"Brrt?" Annie trotted over from her cat bed.

He chuckled at their attention.

"It turned out to be some senior citizens who were upset at the club raising their fees by thirty percent."

"That's a steep hike," Zoe commented.

"Yeah." He nodded.

"What did they do with all the mallets?" Lauren asked.

"Brrt!" *Yes, what?*

"They hid them in the woods nearby, along with the balls, pegs, and hoops."

"Martha wasn't involved, was she?" Lauren asked.

"No." He chuckled. "But I could see her doing something like that."

"Definitely." Zoe nodded.

"Didn't the club think to look for the equipment in the woods?" Lauren crinkled her brow.

"They did, but the members camouflaged them with broken branches and leaves. The club is short staffed at the moment, so the employees didn't have a lot of time to do a thorough search."

"What's going to happen to the culprits?" Lauren wanted to know.

"Not much. Apparently, they've been members for years and management didn't realize how the price increase would affect them. They've come to an arrangement with them – and all the other participants. They'll increase the fees by ten percent this year, instead of thirty, but they might have to increase them by another ten percent next year, depending on their expenses. They're also going to mark up the price of drinks and snacks by a small amount."

"Is anyone going to be arrested?" Zoe asked.

"Brrt?"

"No." Mitch chuckled. "They've apologized and shown management where they hid the equipment, in case anyone else tries this in the future. It's all good."

"That's a relief," Lauren said.

"Yeah, now you can help Detective Castern catch the killer," Zoe said. "Before we do!"

***

Lauren's mother called that night.

"I'd love you and Annie to visit me tomorrow. Zoe, too. Why don't the three of you come over for dinner?"

"Are you sure?" Lauren sat on the couch, Annie nestled beside her.

"Of course. Your father will be there as well, and you can update us in person with your wedding planning."

"Have you received the invitation yet?" She'd posted them yesterday morning.

"Not yet. Hopefully tomorrow," her mother replied.

"Okay." Lauren nodded, although she knew her mom couldn't see her. "I can bring Annie's dinner with me."

"That would be lovely, dear. Can Mitch make it?"

"No." He'd already told her he'd been put on another case, this time involving petty thefts at the supermarket.

"Well, never mind. We can go over the wedding preparations with you and Zoe, as well as Annie." She chuckled.

"Who were you talking to?" Zoe wandered into the living room and sat on the other side of Annie.

Lauren explained.

"Ooh, I like Aunt Celia's cooking." Her eyes lit up. "It sounds like a good idea."

"I guess."

Zoe reached over and patted Lauren's arm. "I thought your mom was okay about you not having the wedding in the knot garden at Stately Vue Hall, especially after … you know."

"She is."

"I know – you don't want her to go dress shopping with you!" Zoe jumped up and pointed at Lauren.

"Mmm." Lauren nodded. She loved her mom, but she'd already thought of buying her wedding gown as something special with just her and Zoe. Sometimes her mother noticed her figure flaws very easily.

"Don't worry. We won't mention our plans for Saturday. If she asks, you can say you're thinking about it, which is true."

"Okay." Lauren felt happier. It would be good to see her parents. She looked down at Annie. "Want to visit Grandma tomorrow?"

"Brrt!"

***

The next afternoon, Lauren's phone buzzed just as she bolted the glass and oak door to the café.

She answered, mystified when Elizabeth's voice sounded on the other end.

"I don't really think—" but Elizabeth cut her off.

"I have a proposition to put to you," the other woman said persuasively. "I promise it will be worth your while. Can you make it this evening?"

"I'm having dinner in Sacramento tonight," Lauren replied, making a face at Zoe, who looked at her curiously.

"That's perfect! Stop in here on the way."

Reluctantly agreeing, Lauren ended the call.

"Who was it?" Zoe wanted to know.

"Brrt?" Annie had left her basket and stood in front of Lauren, her green eyes expectant.

"Elizabeth. She wants me to stop by Stately Vue Hall for some reason. She said she has a proposition *'worth my while'*."

"Ooh." Zoe's eyes lit up. "I wonder what it could be."

"She can be very persuasive." Lauren grimaced. "Mitch and I have already chosen the bistro as our venue."

"And you're thrilled about it. I know." Zoe nodded. "Maybe she wants to pay us to find out who killed her ex-husband!"

"Why would she do that?"

"Because she's disgusted at the fact that Detective Castern hasn't found the killer yet."

"Don't you mean *you're* disgusted?"

"That too," Zoe agreed.

"But how would she even know that we've done some digging around in other cases?"

"Maybe someone told her," Zoe mused. "Another bride who's getting married? Not Brooke, who's doing our hair for your wedding, because she's holding her reception somewhere else. Maybe our sleuthing success has spread past Gold Leaf Valley!" Zoe looked thrilled at the thought.

Lauren suspected the reason Elizabeth wanted to see her was more prosaic.

After cleaning the café, giving Annie a small snack, and freshening up, Lauren checked the time. Almost six.

"I hope we're not going to be late," she fretted as they got into the car, Annie sitting in her carrier in the back, something she wasn't happy about.

"What time is your mom expecting us?"

"Seven for seven-thirty."

"I'm sure she'll understand if we're a little tardy."

"I'll text her with an ETA after we talk to Elizabeth."

When they arrived at Stately Vue Hall, the parking lot was empty.

"Park here," Zoe ordered, pointing to the space closest to the front door.

Lauren did so, then helped Annie out of her carrier and attached the leash to her lavender harness.

As they approached the ornate door, it opened before them.

"Lauren, and Zoe." Elizabeth gave them a welcoming smile, which dropped when she saw Annie. "Oh, dear, you've brought your cat."

"We're a package deal," Lauren told her. The evening air was warm, and she wasn't going to leave Annie in the car, even with the windows down.

"Where we go, Annie goes," Zoe added.

"Well, I suppose." Elizabeth ushered them into the large reception room where they'd had their first meeting.

Once they were seated, Annie sitting demurely on the polished wooden floor next to Lauren's feet, Elizabeth tapped her pen on her clipboard.

"The reason I asked you here is because I have a wonderful proposal for you. I'd love you to have your wedding reception here, and I want to give you a huge discount." She smiled, as if bestowing a great honor upon Lauren.

"Thank you, but—"

"You can even have a Saturday – this year!"

"Wow," Zoe commented.

"Yes. You see—" Elizabeth leaned over the table toward them "—unfortunately we've had some cancellations, since Reginald's death became public knowledge." She frowned. "And that police detective still hasn't caught the killer." She tutted. "But since your fiancé is a detective, I'm sure you wouldn't be fazed at having your wedding here. I'll even upgrade you to a better menu package at no extra cost." She sat back in her chair, as if expecting Lauren to thank her.

"That's kind of you," Lauren began awkwardly, "but we've already found another venue."

"You have?" Elizabeth frowned. "Did I mention that I have connections with a bridal magazine, and I can get you and your groom featured? I think he would be very photogenic."

"So would Lauren," Zoe said indignantly.

"Brrt!"

"Of course, of course," Elizabeth said hastily. "You'll be a beautiful bride. But—"

"I'm sorry, but we've already booked the other venue," Lauren said.

"And the menu is awesome, and Annie will be allowed."

Lauren nodded. Joe, the owner of the bistro, had confirmed that earlier that week.

"That's too bad." A look of annoyance passed over Elizabeth's face. "I was sure you would be happy to take my offer. Not many brides get featured in a magazine."

"What about Brianna?" Zoe asked. "I bet she'd love to be in a magazine."

"Yes, I'm already in talks with the editor about Brianna. She will be our deluxe high-end wedding. But the editor said she'd like a more ordinary couple to be in the feature as well, to inspire other brides-to-be."

"Ordinary?" Zoe frowned. "Lauren is not ordinary. Neither is Annie. Or Mitch."

“You aren’t, either. Or Chris.” Lauren replied. Zoe had always been her greatest cheerleader. She hoped she was Zoe’s.

“I didn’t mean to offend you,” Elizabeth replied. “In fact, just the opposite. Wouldn’t you like other brides to aspire to be like you?”

Lauren knew her mother would be more than pleased if she was featured in a magazine, but she didn’t know if she wanted her life to be available for public consumption like that. Besides …

“I’m sorry, but Mitch and I are happy with keeping our reception local.” More than happy.

“I can see you’ve made up your mind.” Elizabeth handed her a card. “If anything changes in the next week, please call me. That’s when the magazine editor needs a definite answer.”

They rose.

“By the way,” Zoe said innocently, “we bumped into Myrna this week at George’s real estate office. She said she was looking for a condo.”

"Oh, yes." Elizabeth nodded. "She asked for some time off, and since it's quiet here right now—" she grimaced, "—I agreed. Her aunt left her some money." She checked her watch. "She's out looking for a condo again right now. Apparently, there's a new development she found out about today and she might be able to get a good deal if she buys before they're built."

"Is George giving her a big discount?" Zoe asked innocently.

Elizabeth looked taken aback. "I wouldn't know anything about that. You'd have to ask him." She glanced at her watch. "If you'll excuse me, I have another appointment I need to prepare for."

She ushered them out of the building and went back inside.

"I don't think Elizabeth is the killer," Zoe muttered. "If she killed Reginald because George bribed her, it mustn't have been a lot of money, or else she wouldn't be worried about a few cancellations, would she?"

"Unless there are a *lot* more cancellations than she let on," Lauren murmured. "Didn't Myrna tell us that this place is expensive to run?"

"I didn't see any flowers just now like the ones in Reginald's nose and mouth," Zoe continued.

"I didn't, either."

"Has Mitch said anything about the rose petal Annie found here the day Reginald was killed?"

"Just that it's from an ordinary red rose, like the ones in the knot garden." He'd told her over the phone.

"Brrt!"

The roar of a sports car alerted Lauren and Annie. A fancy black car parked next to Lauren's, and George, Brianna's dad, clambered out. He wore dark gray slacks, and a matching shirt.

"I know you." He nodded genially to Lauren, glanced at Zoe, and then down at Annie. "You're getting married here."

"No," Lauren replied.

"We're – Lauren – is getting married in Gold Leaf Valley, and she's having the reception at the bistro there," Zoe said. "It's going to be amazing!"

"Good, good." He nodded. "Bobby said you came in this week to find a new home. Here's my card. Call me anytime and I'll find exactly what you're looking for." He tried to pull a card case out of his pants' pocket, but it got stuck.

"Darn thing. I need to get the lining fixed on this pocket," he grumbled. "I can get you a good deal on a new condo development. Just say the word." He tugged the case free. A couple of dried red rose petals came with it and fell on the ground.

"Brrt!" Annie pounced on them.

Lauren froze, then looked carefully at Zoe. Her cousin looked as shocked as she did. The petals matched the one Annie had found on the day of Reginald's death.

"We've been wrong all along," Zoe said. She pointed at George. "*You* killed Reginald!"

"What? Of course I didn't," he blustered.

"Then why did you have rose petals in your pocket?" Lauren asked.

"The same ones that were stuffed in Reginald's mouth and nose." Zoe shuddered. "I saw them up close."

"And they look just like the one Annie found later that day inside," Lauren added.

"You girls are crazy." He shook his head and attempted to walk past them. "Forget about me giving you a good deal on a condo. You're on your own."

"How much did you bribe Elizabeth or Myrna so Brianna could have her dream date on Saturday, August fourteenth?" Lauren asked, too angry to be scared at confronting a killer.

"Brrt!"

"That cat." He scowled at Annie. "All Brianna can talk about is getting a cat just like yours. On, and on, and on. First she wanted to marry Bobby and be the first girl in her sorority to get married, and now she wants a cat. I'll be glad when this wedding is over."

"It won't be long," Zoe told him. "August fourteenth is only a few weeks away."

"You might be featured in a magazine article," Lauren commented. "Elizabeth was just telling us about it."

"Everything would have been fine if Reginald had given me what I wanted." His eyes narrowed. "No one gets away with crossing me."

Lauren, Annie, and Zoe exchanged a glance.

"Exactly how *did* he cross you?" Zoe asked.

"I had an agreement with Elizabeth. He found out about it and tried to cancel it. Ha!" He pointed a finger at them. "I got the better of him!"

"How?" Zoe persisted.

"By killing him?" Lauren guessed.

He scowled. "Never you mind."

Another car pulled up with a spurt of gravel – a white sports car with only room for two. Brianna was driving, and Bobby accompanied her.

She got out of the car, dressed in a cute but no doubt expensive gold and white sundress, Bobby following in office attire.

"Daddy, the wedding cake has been cancelled! The baker said he was only doing it as a favor to Reginald, but since Reginald is dead, he said he's too busy to make it for me! He says he's an *artist* and he can't deal with me!" She looked indignant. "Daddy, I need you to go and tell him to make me the best cake ever! And then I need you to—"

"Go inside with Bobby." George appeared to be holding on to his temper.

"But Daddy," there was a whine in Brianna's voice, "I need you to—"

"Go. Inside." He bit off each word.

"Fine." She flounced off. Bobby trailed behind her awkwardly.

"You see what I have to deal with?" George pointed a finger at them. "It never stops. *She* never stops. Daddy, fix this. Daddy, fix that. I thought she'd be so busy planning her wedding she'd leave me alone for a while, but *no*. Now there are problems with the wedding. First, she had to have her dream date in August – I have no idea why, except it's a date she's been fixated on since she was twelve and started making her first bridal scrap book. Now the baker has cancelled on her and I have to fix that. Tomorrow it will be some other problem that only *I* can deal with. ARGGH!" He looked like he wanted to pull out his short tufts of hair by the roots.

"So you killed Reginald," Zoe said, "because he was standing in your way."

"Yeah," he confessed after a second. "I needed to get some peace. I'd done a secret deal with Elizabeth to get that stupid dream date in August. But Reginald found out and cancelled it! Can you believe that? I even offered him the same amount I gave to Elizabeth – ten thousand – but he refused!" He snorted. "Reginald said it was unethical and Stately Vue Hall did not partake in such conduct. *Partake*!" George looked like he wanted to spit. "That's the word he used."

"So you killed Reginald and the deal with Elizabeth went ahead?" Lauren guessed.

"Yeah. I think she was so grateful for the money she didn't ask any awkward questions, and didn't want to suspect me, either."

"How did you kill him?" Lauren asked, holding her breath. Elizabeth, and Brianna and Bobby hadn't come outside. Did they even suspect what was going on?

"After he told me I couldn't have that dream date in August – and it was just the two of us at that meeting – he said he had to go out to the knot garden and pick some flowers as he wasn't happy with the ones Elizabeth had chosen that morning. Said they weren't balanced correctly or some garbage. If you ask me, I've done Elizabeth a favor by killing him."

"So Reginald went out to the garden," Zoe prompted.

"Yeah. I followed him, trying to reason with him, but he refused to listen. He just said there would be no deal and that was final. So I decided to show him what was final! I pushed him up against that statue, banged his head against it a couple of times, grabbed some of the flowers he'd just picked, and crammed them into his nose and mouth so he'd be good and dead, then stuffed him upside down into the hedge."

"What about the rose petals in your pocket, and the one Annie found inside?" Lauren asked.

"When I was walking back to the hall, I noticed a few petals on my shirt, so I stuffed them into my pants' pocket." He grimaced. "When I got home, I forgot that the inside lining was frayed and there could be some hiding in there. I pulled out the petals from my pocket, flushed them, and thought I'd got rid of them all – it's not like I counted them. I had no idea there were still some stuck in the lining. I thought I was being smart, not leaving a trail of petals leading back to the house."

"And the rose petal Annie found inside?" Zoe probed.

"Brrt!"

"I guess it must have been stuck on my shoe. The ground was damp out there."

"And it dropped off onto the carpet inside," Lauren surmised.

"I guess." He shrugged. "So, now that you know, how much to keep you quiet?" He pulled out his checkbook. "One hundred, two hundred?"

"Dollars?" Zoe wrinkled her nose. "We don't take bribes."

"I'm talking six figures."

"Brrt?"

"That's right. Two hundred thou for the three of you – you can share it." He chuckled. "I bet that's more than you make in five years – all of you."

"We are not for sale." Lauren straightened her shoulders.

"Yeah." Zoe nodded. "We put people like you away!"

"Brrt!" *That's right!*

"If you're not going to be sensible, then I'll have to deal with you just like I dealt with Reginald." He glanced down at Annie. "Except for the cat. I'll give her to Brianna and then she'll stop yacking about getting one."

"There are three people just inside." Lauren pointed behind her to the ornate front door, hoping her hand wasn't shaking.

"And they haven't come out, have they? My daughter is probably telling Elizabeth all about the nasty baker who's cancelled the cake. Well, let Elizabeth earn her money tonight."

He lunged toward them.

Lauren, Annie, and Zoe shared a panicked look, then at the same time, noticed a coil of garden hose nearby. As George reached for Lauren, Zoe zipped to the right, and Lauren and Annie sprang to the left.

Zoe uncurled the hose and shook it out across the gravel, right in front of George. Lauren bent down and held it tight, noticing Zoe doing the same.

"Brrt!" Annie darted out in front of him, on the other side of the hose, as if daring him to come after her. He took the bait.

"ARRGH!"

George didn't notice the hose acting as a tripwire, and fell to the ground. "My knee, my knee!" He sprawled on his back, one of his knees in the air at an awkward angle.

"Daddy!" Brianna rushed out of the house, followed by Bobby and Elizabeth. She glared at Zoe and Lauren. "What have you done?"

"He tried to kill us." Zoe placed her hands on her hips and returned her glare – with interest.

"That's right." Lauren's legs felt a little wobbly. She reached down and stroked Annie, immediately feeling better. "Thank you," she murmured to her fur baby, glad she was unharmed.

"Brrt." *You're welcome.* She licked Lauren's hand, her tongue sandpapery rough, but comforting.

"I'm calling the police." Elizabeth held a cell phone.

"Good idea," Lauren told her.

"Yeah, you can also tell them how you accepted a bribe from him so Brianna could have her dream date on August fourteenth," Zoe added.

"What happened with the couple who originally booked that date?" Lauren asked curiously.

"I offered them an excellent deal if they took that vacant Tuesday in October," Elizabeth replied. "And I don't regret doing so. It was just business. Do you have any idea how much this place costs to run?"

"So you didn't care you did a deal with a murderer?" Zoe demanded.

"Brrt!"

"What?" Elizabeth looked shocked. "What are you talking about?"

"George—" Zoe pointed to him, still sprawled on the ground "—killed Reginald because he found out about your secret deal and was going to cancel it."

Elizabeth paled. "No! That can't be!"

"Daddy?" Brianna's blue eyes rounded. "Tell them it isn't true!"

"Sir?" Bobby asked. "Can I help you get up?"

"It might be best if we leave him like that until the paramedics arrive," Zoe said.

"Yes," Lauren agreed. She glanced at Elizabeth. "Have you made that call?"

"Oh." Elizabeth's fingers shook as she dialed.

While they waited for help to arrive, George roared at his daughter to stay away from him. Brianna looked hurt.

"I know you couldn't kill anyone, Daddy. Tell them it isn't true!"

When he remained silent, she added, "But Daddy, what about my wedding? Who's going to attend if you're in jail?"

"Arggh!" George pressed his hands against his ears. "Make her stop – please!"

"But Daddy—"

Elizabeth led her inside, Bobby looking bewildered, but obediently following.

"You see?" George removed his hands from his ears. "All my life that's what I've had to put up with. Daddy this, Daddy that. No wonder my wife left!"

"When was that?" Zoe asked, as the roar of sirens grew near.

"When she was just a baby. I tried to make up for it by giving Brianna whatever she wanted, but I just turned her into a spoiled brat instead. And now I'm stuck with her! No wonder her Mom left! Maybe she knew how Brianna would turn out and that's why she ran away."

Squad cars pulled up, along with an ambulance. The trio stepped aside so the paramedics could check George over before loading him onto a stretcher.

A uniformed officer approached them, and they told him that Detective Castern was in charge of the case, although Lauren wished it was Mitch. It would be good to see him right now.

After they gave their statements, they were allowed to go home. Just as they were about to get into their car, Brianna ran outside.

"Daddy!" The ambulance stopped reversing.

Brianna rushed to the back doors and banged on them. They opened slowly.

“Daddy, what am I going to do? Daddy, what about the wedding? Daddy—”

The ambulance doors closed, shutting her out.

“Brianna?” Bobby approached her tentatively. “What can I do to help? I could—”

“Shut up, Bobby. I need to think. Daddy’s not here anymore.” She angrily wiped her eyes.

Lauren settled Annie into her carrier, not wanting to see any more of that scene

“Brrt?” Annie asked softly.

“We’re going to Grandma’s house for dinner,” she replied, feeling a rush of gratitude for her own parents.

“Yeah. A totally normal dinner with my normal aunt and uncle. I can’t wait!”

EPILOGUE

The next day, Mitch updated them at the café during the after-lunch lull.

"George made a full confession at the hospital," he told them. "Apparently, once he started talking, he couldn't stop. He also asked them to ban Brianna from visiting him in hospital. He said he couldn't deal with her right now."

"How is his knee?" Lauren asked. The four of them sat at a table in the rear.

"He's got a badly torn ligament. He should be out of hospital in a couple of days, and then he'll be going to jail, even if he does have a fancy attorney." He paused. "Detective Castern got a little reprimand from our boss for not looking at George and his daughter more closely."

"Good." Lauren nodded in satisfaction.

"Brrt!"

"What about Brianna?" Zoe asked curiously.

Mitch shrugged. "George said she had nothing to do with the murder, or knew anything about it. And by what you told me about her reaction to finding out yesterday, I think that's true. I've heard that he's going to bar her from visiting him in jail, too. Said it's the only way he'll get some peace and quiet."

"Is she still going ahead with the wedding?"

"I haven't heard that she – or Bobby – have called it off yet."

"I hope Bobby will be okay," Zoe said. "He seemed like a nice guy."

"Yes. I don't think he's interested in Brianna because of her dad's money," Lauren added.

"This sort of thing puts you off wanting kids." Zoe shuddered.

What about you?" Mitch took Lauren's hand and looked at her intently.

She smiled at him with certainty. "Ours wouldn't be like that. Not with you as their dad."

"Or with you as their mom." He smiled at her tenderly.

"If you two are going to be all lovey-dovey, I might as well hang out at the counter with a marshmallow latte." Zoe rose. "But I know you two are going to be super awesome parents – one day. Aren't they, Annie?" She winked at the silver-gray tabby.

"Brrt!"

THE END

Made in the USA
Coppell, TX
14 September 2021

62375554R00142